DEEP SLEEP

P.L.U.M READERS

DEEP SLEEP

DyAnna Durbin

DEEP SLEEP

P.L.U.M READERS

This book is a work of fiction. Names, characters, places, and incidents either are products of the author's imagination or are used fictitiously. Any resemblance to actual events or locales or persons, living or dead, is entirely coincidental.

ISBN-13: 978-0-615-30633-9
ISBN-10: 0-615-30633-0

For information regarding bulk purchases, please contact P.L.U.M. Readers at www.plumreaders.com

Acknowledgements

As always, I am indebted to my mother, Mildred, who believed in me; and to my children; Darrell, Jr. and Amber, for their patience.

Special thanks to Jacqueline Rainey, Angel Melaine and Dianne DeVaughn.

DEEP SLEEP

PROLOGUE

There will be a point in time when evil reveals itself, holding its own hostages to stand trial for its failing manifestation on earth, and then released. Released among the dead and living, the good and the bad, projecting their precise conclusions followed by the roads it travels. We do not know how and when these conclusions will emerge, but a judgment day will come and blindly smear their intersections without warning.

An imprint of our past can tell stories of locked up moments, and once unlocked, it can change our lives forever. There will be moments when fate passes through time, lining up chain-of-events and shifting the roads of life in unparalleled directions.

INTRODUCTION

Before eighteen hundred, a half a century ago, Columbus came ashore. The Atlantic Coast was a virgin. The coastal waters of South Carolina stroked this land mass for miles, preserving its new embryo. Then it gave birth to Beaufort; a sea island nurtured by the shoal waters. Beaufort, South Carolina entered maturity by the mid 1800's where mansions were built by the wealthy owners of cotton, indigo, and rice plantations.

Beaufort found prosperity by those generations who supported slavery to preserve their newfound golden inheritance; Africans. However, these Africans were strangers to this foreign land. Stolen from their motherland and stripped of their heritage, some survived the deplorable conditions while others were coerced to some dubious method of suicide. Slaves close to the sea or rivers were more likely to escape by water, if they could indeed escape.

A diverse southern-coast dialect was adopted on land, keeping Africans traditions and customs of their homeland.

Their religious style of worship reflected their cultural heritage, along with a spiritual life. They believed in the dual nature of the soul and spirit. In death, one's soul returns to God, but the spirit remains on earth living among the individual's descendants.

Beaufort held many dark secrets surrounding its womb of African survivors and its settlers. Still, there are some mysterious breaths that breathe the past, and they cannot hushed nor buried. It inhales and exhales the flesh it holds in contempt. Until that flesh attempts to reveal its voice, dusk will mask the night without sight.

On the morning of June 25, 2007, ten years after being with the company, Joel Lee Keys is sweating like an icicle that can't be licked quickly enough. Promotions were about to be announced and the idea of not knowing his fate with the company, if any, kept the blood from flowing to his white knuckles. Joel, a senior civil architect, worked for one of the largest growing architect firms in Atlanta, Georgia.

Consequently, the firm was going to open another office in Savannah, Georgia. A year ago, Joel inherited 72 acres of land in Beaufort, South Carolina, a small island that bonds with the Atlantic Ocean. He never had any interest in it, but on this day, he will.

Never in a million years would Joel have thought his life would change with one dream. Nor was he prepared for the burdens that went along with his inheritance.

One

BEAUFORT, SOUTH CAROLINA-1943

Under the sounds of buzzing horse flies and chirping crickets, a fragile voice whispered. "Ah knows yuh down dare." The soft voice, spoke again, "Ah know you can see me too." Eyes wide open, Lula tried not to hear herself breathe; she clearly listened out for every wave's echo. Her obsession with the wave's salsa was quite visible. It was only then, she believed the deep waters celebrated her company.

DEEP SLEEP

On August 29, 1943 Lula turned thirteen years old. Her tawny eyes pierced the open Atlantic with her reminiscence. Of her memories, the ones she had, she brought it with her here, on the edge of the splintered dry-rotted dock where the water and the state of South Carolina coalesced. Lula grins and giggles to herself as though she were not alone. "It's my birthday...It's my birthday." In that joyous moment, she closed her eyes then inhaled the one thing that soothed her emotions, the deep-sea's mist.

The saline ocean's mild wind blew on her face as the sun blanketed a comfort of warmth over her naked skinny legs. She snuggled her bald fists under her maturing breasts to keep them from flattening down against the dock's hard surface. Lula stared downward into the murky water and spoke again. "God done gave me another year tuh be witcha." She continued to talk to the ocean, and the ocean talked back with symphony-sounding waves that splashed against the beams holding the offshore dock.

Regardless of emotional cultural differences, Lula was meant to be born in Beaufort, South Carolina. As she grew older, she appreciated the country and enjoyed the affection of hospitality. At times, her perception of the south was like living in a colorblind world. Her southern tongue expressed a refreshed tone; it was like discovering a new language.

Meagerly living the 'American Dream' day to day, she and her mother worked for a white family. The family was not rich, but had enough money to hire Lula and her mother, Rosa Lee, as domestic servants. All together, Lula and Rosa Lee brought home eight dollars a week for five days' work. Following the death of Lula's father, the family suffered sorrow, bitterness and fear. That pain brought them to move in with Rosa Lee's mother.

Every so often, Lula couldn't seem to keep a sheen of tears from glossing over her eyes at the thought of her father. Those tears brought her to the water's edge.

Back at the dock, Lula unfolded her thin arms and hung them down over the edge. Her gaze entered the ocean's door, contemplating on what's beyond the water's surface, her reflection welcomed her. In confidence, she explored memories with every thought, emotion and moment of peace, gifted by the deep over the years. Her soul dipped into the water. Strength for life was abundantly released through the fossils and sand swirling around her. The blackness guarded her. Fearlessly, she roamed, without a care in the world. Lula floated with composure, both arms out by her side, unlocking her golden-brown eyes wide. She spoke, "Show yo' face."

Staring forward into the deep, Lula comes to be sluggish. Almost like, she was coming out of a trance.

Suddenly an exploding force pressed through the sea and disturbance flowed all around. Lula was pinned in a whirlwind, descending to the ocean's floor. "Lemme go!" She screamed in horror. Seconds later, Lula continuously blinked her eyes, heart beating rapidly; chest rising above her shoulders, she rolled over to her face and looked out at a shadow howling out her name. "Lula...Lula!"

It was Rosa Lee—a fleshy one hundred and eighty pounds, 5'3", bowlegged woman hastily marching, swaying one arm backward and forward, with one hand placed on her hips. Every step she took, she wiped the relentless sweat seeping through her scalp off, running down her sapped face. It was as if someone poured a bucket of water over Rosa Lee's head and curled the edges of her thick, crimped ground-pepper hair in knots. Even though, she always kept her hair in one plait, wrapped in a bun with a barrette, she had to wash it every other day because the summer sweat made her hair stink like a clammy mop.

Standing by the walkway of the dock between the tall straw grass, she called out to Lula again, "Lula...Lula come nah!" Rosa Lee continued in her stride closer to Lula, muttering to herself, "Ah'd told dis gal tuh stay away from heah...Ah know she hears me." As Rosa Lee came upon Lula lying across the ridged dock, she noticed Lula was dripping wet. She scolded her for swimming on a day like today. "Chile you lost yo' mind. Here, Ah'm swetin fuh you on yo' birthday and you swim in de only decent fabric you own!" Rosa Lee lifted Lula up by her arm like a Raggedy Ann doll, "Didn't Ah tell yuh tuh never come over heah!" Eyeballing each other, one demanded an answer, the other dazed in silence, for she knew any word said the wrong way would mean a horse strap across her narrow butt. Tightly clutching Lula's arm, Lula walked away from the soil-less garden that gave her unknown forces beyond the earth's capability.

"Momma, huccome we ain't made tuh live unda wader?"

An already upset Rosa Lee, somewhat stunned and confused at Lula's question, responded, "Whatcha yuh mean?"

Lula asked again, "How'd come we ain't made tuh live in wader?"

Rosa Lee, still puzzled, answered, "Cuz God made it dat way...besides we'd drown. Nah gal go'n in de house, put some dry clothes on and fix yo'self up for yo' birthday dinner." She laughed, almost as puzzled as she looked.

Lula paused before entering the cracked, painted, framed screen door of her grandmother's house and turned around to look at Rosa Lee. "Momma Ah wunt drown."

Rosa Lee looks at Lula with sincerity and says, "Baa'buh Ah knows it."

"Yeah yuh would," interrupted by a brash voice, rushing out the screen door. It was Joseph, Lula's oldest brother. At birth, he weighed nine pounds and six ounces, and it took three midwives to assist with his birth. Not to mention, Rosa Lee's sexual organ was torn and had to get seven stitches. Joseph's head was bigger than his body. Every day, Rosa Lee would mold his head with her hands. She gradually shaped his head until his body caught up with it. Joseph was the spitting image of his father. If you didn't look long enough, you weren't sure if it were him or James. By the time Joseph reached fifteen, he was as tall as his father, standing six feet with broad shoulders. Their appearance was mysteriously dark, and you couldn't tell if they were sweating until it dripped off their faces.

Mr. James Kannon was a Beaufort, South Carolina native, having been born and raised in the backwoods approximately twenty miles from the Atlantic's shoreline. His parents' parents, and more generations since the early 1800's had been bought and sold at the sea ports of Beaufort.

In spite of Beaufort's cultural tensions, James was more, or less respected around Beaufort. Early Europeans of Beaufort bragged to one generation after another about how they captured an African leader, and members of a distinct military tribe, and discovered gold. The story of James's great, great, great-grandfather was recorded and tucked away in the minds of Beaufort folks, who carefully maintained what was thought of the olden times and didn't dare to challenge it. Any acknowledgement of James's noble lineage was smothered in conversations, as though, it was unheard of.

James was a descendant of King Matura Tutu of a great West African kingdom. While some members of the nation were sold on the coast of Georgia in 1888, King Tutu's birth name was stripped away along with is his heritage on the seaports of Beaufort. Eventually, his identity died on land. James's great, great-grandfather, Khufa Tutu, who was now renamed Abram Kannon, relentlessly denounced the forced life of slavery. In the dusk of night, where no one could see or hear him speak to his people, he reminded them of Africa's burning deserts, green mountains, lush and majestic rivers. These descriptive sceneries stayed alive in Abram for many years. He was determined to die with his sovereign heritage fastened to his bare back. Long ago, on the edge of night, where numerous stars gave flare to the sky, Abram Kannon spoke for the last time.

"We mus' hol' on to our spiritual beliefs by doin' wut we 'own fo 'farduhs did by leaven dis' unholy land. Ah'll not be made tuh see mah mudduh, sistuh, wife and daa'tuh raped, nuh beatin'. Ah'll not stand by and watch mah fadduh, brudduh, and sons hung and viciously whipped 'til breath is no longer a gasp...no man should endure dese crimes upon dare

families by 'nother man. Dis land wunt bound our souls fuh'ever..."

James every now and then recited similar old stories passed down to his father, from his grandfather. *"When Ah wuz growin' up, mah dadduh told me things dat would make yo' hair stand up...We'd come from kings and queens dat owned green pastures seen beyond eye sights, as far as mountain tops, all da way 'cross da earth down tuh de waders and back on land again. He use tuh say, 'Know yo' enemies befo' dey become enemies, and alwaze remember dere's uh price on everything, and 'cause yuh have a heart, at times dat'll cost too.'* James would take a long pause in the middle of his story telling, and then quickly start up again. *"Dadduh use tuh say, 'Our fo'folks tears and blood drops were healed by songs of self-strength dat came wid de linin' of dare souls. Dis soil dat sucks in mah sweat and holds me up every day has many powers buried from mah kin'folks. Dey vanished mysteriously one night. Dey left 'cuz dey were stolen from dem'own hope and wanted tuh set up ground fuh de unbound future of our generation. Dadduh said dare wuz a curse on dis land dat tried to stop us from bein' bound by one, but another power greater kept our people buildin' unda dis sky."*

Lula and Joseph never questioned their father, not even if they were curious about something he said—they were taught to listen. Although Lula always loved

8

listening to her father's family history, Joseph was reluctant to receive any information that was going to do him any good. Many times, Joseph's eyes would drift away from the direction of his father's voice, but a heavy finger-flick on the top of his forehead always brought his attention back. James and Rosa Lee knew Joseph was going to be slow six months after birth - yet they never mentioned it to anyone. As a young boy, Joseph's reactions to certain things weren't always on the mark. If you took your index finger and moved it across his eyes to the right, he would look to the left.

In front of Lula's grandmother house, Rosa Lee gripped her forty-eight inches of hips and said, "Joseph, hush yo' mouth and git back here wit mah flour, yuh heah me?"

Lula paid no heed to her brother's remark and continued to walk in the house. She slowly paced herself across the fractured floor into the bedroom where she shared with her mother. Her body stood in front of the ebony-framed mantle mirror, motionless, holding up her silence. Her eyes drifted, still attached to the swaying of the ocean's melody. Staring at her dripping wet arms and legs, she stepped closer to the mirror, feeling somehow she had just witnessed an unknown world. A paranormal presence had passed through her reflection from the deep into her soul. Not afraid of herself, Lula touched the glass. In that moment, her fears and uncertainties were abandoned. She turned thirteen today and shared the one thing that pacified her heart, the deep.

Two

BEAUFORT, SOUTH CAROLINA-1943

Joseph hit the turf with his untied boots covered with gunk, on his way to get Rosa Lee's flour. The general store, now and then known as the big-box store, was the only store located within ten miles off the coast of Beaufort. Though it was a small shack, it carried a wide selection of goods for Beaufort's residents.

The store's owner was Adam Creech. Everyone called him "Ole man Creech." He had two sons that weren't worth a back scratch. Gabe and Seth were their names. Spoiled rotten to the core, they always kept trouble in the air. They wanted to be somebody bigger than who they actually were. Gabe was somewhat shy as a young boy. Seth, the oldest, fought it out of him on a daily basis. Gabe eventually became rotten-minded; lying, stealing and swindling soon befitted his first nature. Not surprisingly, ole man Creech never taught his boys morals or values. He was greedy too. He always made deals or traded with Beaufort folks who didn't have the means of paying him back. So, the people would have to give up their most precious possessions, sometimes their daughters' innocence, to do business. Ole man Creech knew what the folks had before they came to him to ask for help.

Henry Willsworth was an 80-year-old Beaufort native, dumpy with a white nappy colonial beard that covered his front neck. He lost his wife's valuable brooch to ole man Creech in exchange for lumber. Henry knew ole man Creech before he was born a bastard. In 1893, a woman by the name of Mary Bells knocked on Henry's door at three o'clock in the morning; red lipstick ran around her mouth, smudged mascara crud blackened her eyes, and she was sobbing uncontrollably. Loose-legged was the word the townsmen used to describe her. Men in Beaufort couldn't get enough of her and the women despised her.

With child for the third time within a year, she was too late in finding Henry's wife, Sue Willsworth, for an abortion. Henry and Sue were the best-kept secret for women and girls who were in trouble, but were quick to turn them away when the weeks took on a life form.

Needless to say, ole man Creech survived Mary's botched abortion. With the help of Sue, Mary gave birth and bled profusely for twelve days straight until the warm pink in her skin melted. After fifty-four years of hiding what she felt was a sin-filled occupation, Sue died from liver disease. Some say she drank herself to death. After each abortion performed, she consumed an entire flask of whisky.

Henry wanted to give Sue a proper burial and needed more lumber to build the coffin and a wagon to haul it to the burial ground. Henry didn't have as much as necessary, so he asked ole man Creech if he would take his wife's gold brooch in exchange for lumber, and he would repay him with cotton loads from the mill for the next six months. Ole man Creech refused and told Henry, one year of cotton payment, including the gold brooch, and he could get all the lumber needed. Henry agreed.

Three

It was Sunday, August 29, 2007. Feeling good about the promotion and the move to Beaufort, South Carolina, Joel and Holly couldn't wait to get acquainted with their 1980s restored home. Nestled on their 72 acres, the heirloom cottage had three bedrooms, one bath, living, formal dining room, and a wraparound porch. The home looked like a big white box with a black top, except grander. It mounted on short columns of heavy brick and cinder block.

Holly stopped unpacking at sundown to shower while Joel emptied out one of his favorite spirits. He stood in the doorway, smoothly swallowing his vodka, while watching Holly dry off her soft pink, naked body. Her body was tone, and perfectly shaped in all the right places.

"Well, now." He cleared his throat. "I am the luckiest man on earth." Joel sat the shot glass down, his dreamy eyes locked on Holly's butt. Holly bent over with one foot on the edge of the bed and the other adjacent to the floor. Joel untied the strings to his gym shorts; loosely they fell to his ankles.

The night air inhaled and exhaled the white lace curtains in and out of the half-open windows. Across the room, a king-sized bed wore colorless cotton sheets. The bed took up half the space in the room, but Joel didn't care. Joel searched the old room for anything familiar. He swiftly took another swig of his drink and rested the glass on the edge of an aged dresser that came with his inheritance, and slowly caressed Holly's body. He couldn't get enough of Holly. His eyes and imagination went wild. Roughly he molded his body alongside her 8-size figure. He cushioned his face in her breasts, rubbing then smoothing out her behind. Sensuously, Holly shifts her body forward into his pelvis. "I love you," she softly says.

"You will always be my precious *Scarlett*." Joel purrs in Holly's ear.

"I can't believe we actually picked up and moved away. No more sitting in traffic on I-85. What do you say we break in our new life...Let's do a little skinny dipping?"

"Now?" Joel asks.

"Why not? There's no one next door looking out the window. Besides, you are now the proud owner of this beautiful land."

Joel slightly nodded his head and motioned his eyes, yes. Holly jumped out of bed to get towels.

The aging moon beamed fluorescent gold and orange shadows off the ocean. The moist air draped the evening sky with warmth. The sky had no warning of movement below its belly that barely surrounded the old soil lying off the coast.

Joel and Holly romped in the ocean's shallow surf, and the waves became a blanket against their bodies. The darkness grew quiet and Holly took the chance to reveal her deepest feelings for Joel. Holly took deep breaths and wiped the water away from her eyes, turned to Joel slowly and said, "I'm so happy now." Before Joel could utter a word, Holly positioned herself and jumped in his arms, only for him to lock her legs behind his back.

"Me, too," Joel said.

"Dear God, thank you for sending me this man."

"You know what, Holly?"

"What?"

Joel secured Holly's body on his stomach and tilted his head upward to face the nameless stars, and confessed his love openly. "I love Holly O'Connor!" An echo crossed from one rock to another and traveled on top of the ocean, heard through the hollow entrances of sea caves. Holly shrieked, and could not believe Joel actually yelled out his love for her.

"Quiet," Holly shushed Joel. She unlocked her legs from his back. "The whole world hears you."

Joel smiling, looking up to the starlit sky, "That's the point, my dear!"

The smell of marine sea grass was getting stronger in the air, and the water became agitated. All of a sudden, an unexpected chill touched the midnight air and graciously stretched over the ocean like an autumn breeze. Underneath the surface that cradled Beaufort's black sea, selfishly bred higher waves, sucking down every particle floating on its skin.

"Hey, it's getting nippy out here." Joel said while rubbing the cold bumps on his arms.

"It feels fine to me."

As Joel and Holly nibbled on each other's bottom lip, Holly rubbed her hands all over Joel's upper body to keep him warm. Still with disbelief of the abrupt climate change, Joel languorously dropped his head on Holly's right shoulder.

"Are you all right?" Holly asked.

"No. All of a sudden, I don't feel so good." Joel stood motionless, unaware the night was about to get disastrous. Lights that guarded the house and the ocean frontier shattered all at once, unexpectedly.

"What the hell!" Joel confused, turning his head from left to right with fear. "Talk about a blackout." Joel held his arms out to the side with his palms kissing the sky. Still quiet and unsure of his recent discovery, he did not want to scare Holly. But the wind was still, and the shallow water was icing.

"Hey, let's get out of here." Joel calmly suggested. He gently tugged on her arm suggesting that something was clearly wrong. Joel and Holly rushed out of the water to the front porch that had obviously passed its era of plantation life.

"That's strange, the air out here is fine," Joel said.

"Maybe there was an unexpected wind shift?"

"No, maybe the water didn't like us."

"No, you mean the water didn't like you." Holly jokingly said.

Joel fought his unexpected ailment and fell back on the porch stairs holding his gut, trying not to alarm Holly. Holly sat comfortably on the wraparound porch, looking out to the sea and around the land. As she breathes in with relaxing thoughts, she noticed, in the distance, a burning fire and a shadow by it.

"Honey, did you know we have a neighbor?" Holly strained her eyes to get a clearer view.

"Oh yeah, the realtor lawyer said we did. He's an elderly man that's lived in this area for nearly 80 years. I've been meaning for us to say hello, maybe we can do it tomorrow."

"I wonder what it was like living here, back then?" Holly said while imagining to herself.

Joel pulled himself up from the stone steps. "I'm sure you will find out."

Four

The 80-year-old neighbor's cheeks were sucked in with wrinkles so deep that they looked like scribbled line drawings all over his face. Grey-haired, he stood six feet and seven inches tall. His dark russet, spider-webbed eyes could tell stories of fatherless births, unknown deaths, comings and goings of neighbors and travelers who stepped on the shores of Beaufort's sand. A man of few words, he spoke with his extruding eyeballs, known as "Silent Night" by the older town folks. Everyone else knew him as "Ned". Neighbors always knew what Ned meant without him speaking.

Every night, the fire crackled from old, beat up steel barrels full of garbage and wood. It kept him company as he lulled the fire with an old spiritual hymn.

> *"Oh Lord -- Didn't come here to stay, cuz Ah'm gonna meet you at judgement day. Someday you know Ah'd be dere. Oh Lord -- Didn't come here to stay, dere wid you mah heart will not be weary. Ah'm gonna go down by de river and get on mah knees and pray..."*

Holly could not get over the fact that a native was their neighbor. She wanted to make a good impression and extend their hospitality to ensure that they got along peacefully. As Holly puffed the pillows on the bed, she reassured Joel that she was going to say hello to their neighbor.

Joel replied with a smile, "I think he would like that." He walked over to Holly and held her into his heart and said, "Give us a couple of days to get settled in and we can invite him over for dinner." Holly's eyes shimmered.

The next morning squawking sea gulls soared through the sky. Joel leaned forward on the front porch, catching the early mist with his nose. Worriedly he sucked in and out the air beneath the sky. This was the first morning waking up in his inheritance. Joel sipped his coffee with one hand, while his other hand wove through his yellowish brown natural curls. He scanned the ocean with his blue eyes, as though he were controlling the motion of waves, setting them in their rightful place as they rolled onto the shore.

Holly eased up behind him, caressing his firm chest with the palm of her hands. "This is a beautiful place...I bet you can't wait to sink your toes in the sand?"

Joel's voice interrupted the steady breeze blowing on his face. "How did you sleep last night?"

"Like a baby. What about you?"

Less than forty-eight hours since they moved in the house, Joel had a nightmare the night before and didn't want to share it with Holly. In it, a dark figure covered in seaweed slime took him by the hand and led him to the ocean shore. They walked as though the ocean were a fortress. Giant seaweeds were situated like iron gates, while sharks and whales swarmed along their borders. The mucky figure and Joel walked into the watery forest, never stopping and never speaking.

He didn't dare tell Holly about the dream. Holly's mood was serene. Spoiling the mood would have been wrong. Timing was everything. It was in that second, when he stared into Holly's eyes and made that decision.

"I still can't believe we did it. We actually moved out of Atlanta," Holly said gloating.

"Now, we all are kin folks."

DEEP SLEEP

Holly gently slaps Joel in the mouth, "I'm going to cook us a good ol' fashioned country breakfast."

"Fine, just make sure the grits are done this time."

Five

Two days later

It is 2:00 A.M. The ocean is moaning. Joel and Holly calmly slept through the full moon guarding the night. The hundred-year-old Spanish moss trees cover the land, carrying their scent, mixed with the salted draft for miles. Joel and Holly was sound asleep, breathing in and out the night air. Suddenly the mood shifted, and the comfortable night air was unfelt. Without warning, Joel's body came to life and started to become restless. His flesh wouldn't mold to the white sheets of the bed for comfort. Sweat oozed down his scalp through his short, curls clinging like ivy. Wiping excessively, he managed to sit up, mumbling. "Man...it's hot in here."

He sluggishly pulled his body upright and sat on the edge of the bed, exhausted. Barley holding his head up, he gripped the damp sheets to wipe away the sweat from his stinging eyes. Slowly, he gained consciousness and glanced at Holly, peacefully sleeping. He wanted to make certain Holly was breathing, so he recited her name several times for assurance. "Holly...Holly...Holly are you awake?"

"What!" Holly grumbled coming out of her sleep.

"It's burning up in here."

Holly rolled over, her eyes still closed. "You're dreaming."

"Holly, look at me. Does it look like I'm fucking dreaming!" Joel wailed.

Holly opened her eyes and steadily held her attention at Joel's tone of voice. "What's wrong?"

"It's so god damn hot in here!" Beads of sweat poured down his face.

Holly slowly sat up in bed and realized Joel was sincerely struggling with a fever. She held her hands to her face, patting her cheeks, almost slapping herself awake. "Joel, maybe you're coming down with something?"

"It's so fucking hot!"

Holly quickly saw Joel's frustration and got out of bed to comfort him.

"Don't touch me!" Joel angrily shouted as he moved away from her.

"What!" Holly was taken by surprise. "I'm only trying to help you," she says.

"Holly...open the frickin windows!"

Frantically, Holly moved around the bedroom, looking for anything that might have been causing Joel to heat up. She noticed the sheer curtains blowing in and out of the window and the breeze meeting her face.

"Joel, I think you're coming down with the flu or something."

"That's great. Now you're a god damn doctor!" Joel roared.

Holly, stunned by Joel's futile remark, snapped, "Look, I am only trying to help you. There is no need for you to be a smart ass."

"Smart, yes, but the only ass in this house is the ass I fuck!"

She cried, "I can't believe you're talking like this to me. I want to help you."

"You want to help me?" Joel hit his chest with his knotted fists. "Well, Holly darling, you better help yourself." He spit in her direction.

Hastily, Joel started towards Holly, clutching his hands around her neck. She struggled to pry his fingers free. She managed to knee him in his crotch. Immediately, his fingers peeled off her neck. Automatically, he cupped his hands to comfort his manhood that was now in excruciating pain. Holly quickly put distance between them and grabbed Joel's golf club that had been leaning against some unpacked boxes.

"Fuck!" Joel ground his teeth as he pulled up from his crooked pose.

"This is the only ass in the house; now see if you can fuck it." Holly said gripping the golf club and swinging it like a clutch hitter. Holly violently struck Joel's left shoulder then his right. He caught the third strike coming down and snatched the golf club away from her. She stumbled backward and fell over the cardboard boxes, bumping her head against the base of the solid brass coat rack. Panicking, she attempted to slide herself across the floor, placing more distance between them. He continued to move steadily towards her, raising the golf club up in the air.

"You bitch!"

"Joel, please stop! Please Joel...I'm begging you, please stop." Holly pleaded as she continued to slide herself back on the floor.

Joel was not backing down. He started to pace a circular path closer and closer towards Holly. Steadily trembling with rage, a dark shadow in the mirror caught his attention. Abruptly, he stopped in his tracks and turned to view the unknown darkness face to face. Suddenly, the mirror filled with fog until his reflection disappeared. The muscles twitched in his eyes like a finger on the trigger of a gun. Joel's body froze.

Curled up in a corner, desperately trying to catch her breath, Holly noticed that Joel's rigid body was like a statue in the mirror. She swallowed down her wet fears, the size of cotton balls, and ran across the bedroom holding her stomach. Keeping her eyes on Joel, she noticed something strange was happening to him. Joel was glued to the mirror, and the idea of harming Holly didn't seem significant anymore. Holly, still on guard, tiptoed toward the bedroom door. As she moved closer, she quickly opened the door and ran out. Minutes later, she returned and cautiously entered the bedroom with both arms before her, shakingly pointing a 45 semi-automatic gun directly at Joel. Joel never looked away from the mirror. The tranquilizing mirror held Joel hostage, erasing his current surroundings.

"Joel!" Holly shouted, taking one hand off the trigger to wipe away the dripping mucus from her nose. She trembled as she moved behind Joel, "You fucking jerk! I told you to never put your hands on me. What the hell is wrong with you?"

The second hand ticked boorishly on the chrome Westclox sitting on the night stand. Joel's memory left his brain like a whale's insides being snatched out...except there wasn't any bloodshed. Then he collapsed. He laid archways, with his flushed bone cheek against the wooden floor, quivering while saliva discharged down the side of his mouth. Holly noticed and ran to him.

Joel, just like a mouse wedged in a trap, the thought of freedom seemed endless. In the mirror's reflection, Joel appeared in another house that he was unfamiliar with and the surroundings were that of another time. What he saw was not lucid in his mind.

IT'S 1942
JAMES SURPRISED ROSA LEE

"Kids fine'ly got dare own room!" Rosa Lee said grinning all the way back to her ears.

"Dat's not all babbuh. Ah-got yuh somthin' yuh alwaze wanted." Rosa Lee grabbed James' cheeks, kissing them repeatedly. She separates herself quickly and runs to the front porch. A cool breeze from the ocean comes over her caramel skin.

"James ah-knows why yuh build us a haws here."

"Yeah." James knew why too. James' eyes strayed across the land and out to the Atlantic Ocean. Rosa Lee sat down in her gifted rocking chair with a beam of glory seen for miles.

Moments later, Joel came to, exhaling vapors of cold air while he leaked sweat from every pore in his body. Holly noticed a yellowish puddle underneath his butt extending across the floor and knew something was terribly wrong. She fell to him on the floor, struggled to lift up his body into the bathroom. In the end, Joel and Holly eyes made contact, there were no words, only tears.

Six

The next morning, Joel rose from his crippled soul, anxiously waiting for comfort to set in. He surrendered his fear for that moment and wearily walked to the kitchen to make coffee. The kitchen was a country setting of an old southern style. Maintenance for homes on Beaufort plantations became ideal for historians and those who were awarded such inheritance to maintain family legacies.

The kitchen original wood floors were still set in place with a few new wood boards that offset the different shades of pine. Modern fixtures, such as the stove and sink, were white, although the heavy chrome faucet was suffering from hard water stains. The walls were still in good shape, even though the depressed wallpaper was noticeably peeling off throughout the house. There were depictions of preserved crafts left behind by the previous owners. You could tell these crafts have passed down through generations.

As Joel reached over the smooth white, ceramic counter top to pull open the cabinet, he distinctively noticed that one of the picture frames was without glass. It was hanging on the wall adjacent to the cabinet. It had a vintage, rustic, and silver tone barrette with an amethyst purple stone set on it. Just a stare alone was enough for Joel to decide to take the picture down and throw it on the counter top without a momentary look back.

It was shortly after that, he walked out the kitchen recognizing his need to drive to town for groceries.

Joel was getting out of the car in the grocery store parking lot, at the same time, a red corvette pulled up to the driver's side. It was a young woman, who couldn't help but notice his Georgia, Fulton county license plate. She was a cocoa-skinned beauty with a tamed bob cut hairstyle of straight jet-black hair that reached an inch past her chin in front and was shorter in back. Her cheeks were full, chin rounded. Her dark brown eyes, with thick, black brows gave her a distinguished look.

"Welcome to Beaufort," she said.

"Thank you."

"Visiting?"

"No, this is home now."

"A big difference, huh." The young woman smiled.

"You got that right!"

"Let me introduce myself. Hi, my name's Erin."

"Hi, my name's Joel. I moved here from Atlanta. You already know that," chuckled Joel.

"Nice to meet you."

"Likewise."

Joel checked his watch while he walked out the grocery store. He was anxious to get back home. He was still befuddled about the night before.

Gravel crunched beneath the tires as he pulled up in front of the house. He cut off the engine, however, didn't get out. Joel sat still for a moment then leaned his head back against the seat, closed his eyes, and tried to yearn for things to go back to the way they were before last night. A bite dented his bottom lip; he slammed his fist against the steering wheel. "What the hell is wrong with me...?" He began looking forward, eye balling his surroundings with caution. As he swung his legs out, a tall dark man was beside the car door, pulling it the rest of the way open for Joel.

"You need some he'p?"

"Hello." Joel's eyes widened. "I'm sorry, I didn't see you standing there."

"Dat's all right. Do yuh need he'p wid yo' bags."

"No, I think I can handle it."

"Well, all right den, Mista Keys."

"You know my name. How do you know my name?"

"Ah'd met yo' wife a few days ago."

"You're our neighbor."

"Dat's me."

"It's nice to meet you finally." Joel extended his right hand out to shake Ned's hand. Ned returned the shake with a tight gaze.

"Okay den, Ah'll mus' be on my way."

For that moment, Joel instantly forgot his deadlock thoughts.

Seven

On that same morning, as the new sales accountant for a museum featuring exhibits on Beaufort's local history, Holly arrived at work mystified. Hurt from a man she trusted and loved, she couldn't let go of the fact that Joel's fuming behavior almost cost them their lives the night before. She felt as if all the years she spent with Joel had been for nothing. Like waves pounding on rocks, it hit hard and meddled her mind.

Her thoughts were interrupted by a knock on her office door. The idea of faking a happy greeting seemed useless. It was Adrian, a close friend and ex-co-worker from Atlanta. Adrian took on a temporary job assignment as Holly's assistant. His tenure was during the company's merger in 2000. Holly kept Adrian on, due to his energetic potential and punctuality. Adrian's drive to learn beyond his job excited Holly. Eventually, Adrian became Holly's masterpiece and Adrian was Holly's greatest teacher. From the same world and diverse cultures, they had one thing in common – a true friendship.

"Whazzz up?" He was looking forward to surprising Holly at the office; instead, he was met with her unlively welcome. She never lifted her head to acknowledge his face. Adrian realized the poignant look on her face, so he stepped closer to see if she would look up. "Guess who?" Holly's acknowledgement was merely light breath. Adrian's eyes grew curiously. He plumped down in the chair, in front of her desk, "Good morning to you too."

"Shoot, Adrian! I thought you guys were coming in town on Friday."

"Holly, what is wrong with you?" Adrian knew it was Friday, but he didn't bother correcting her. He could see there was something truly aching her.

Holly looked into his eyes with vagueness and wanted to tell him, but she held back and gathered herself together. "Where's Carmen?"

"She decided to do some last minute shopping. You know how you women are!"

"I can't wait to hang out with her again."

"She can't wait either."

"I haven't had my cup of coffee yet."

"You look like you need more than some damn coffee."

Holly stood up, straightened her suit jacket, and smoothed her hair. "Just because we are in another state, you still don't get off owing me money for your curse words, therefore, you still owe me fifty cents."

Adrian realized that Holly's changing of the subject was disconnected and he wasn't going to let her get away with it. "Holly, please talk to me. Did you and Joel have a fight?"

"You know that Joel and I don't fight. Stop trying to get out of owing me fifty cents."

"Holly, you look a mess."

Knowingly, exhausted and disgusted, she was still sensitive. She matted her lips tightly so no air could get in.

"I'm sorry, but you do."

"Thanks a lot," rolling her eyes sideways. She picked up a mirror to view what she already knew. Adrian could not take his eyes off Holly, knowing something was terribly wrong.

"Holly, I'm sorry. I have never seen you like this before, if something is wrong, I want to help. You and Joel are like my big brother and sister, and there's nothing I wouldn't do for you."

"I'm telling you, all I need is my cup of coffee."

"Well, let's go get a cup."

"Only, if you promise to have a cup with me."

Holly led the way and Adrian followed behind her slowly.

Eight

Midafternoon, Joel stood at the foot of the dock quietly thinking about his embarrassing behavior the night before in the bedroom. He tried to make sense of his frightful adventure that had imprisoned him. Like a bloody rat in a trap that's been tightly smashed across its belly, he squirmed. He stared out at the ocean and concealed his sobbing independently by holding his head back and blindly looking up to the sky. It seemed that, the longer he stared out at the ocean, the calmer he was going to feel.

Right then, peace surged all around him, as though his past vile condition was just a state-of-being, a dream of sorts. Without warning, the nearly century-old dock collapsed. Joel shot down into the water. The water steadily sucked his body below. More and more, Joel started swimming upward. The spirited current kept Joel paddling and kicking relentlessly for freedom. Eventually, the sunlight closed up to a tiny circle. The journey to reach the top seemed hopeless, the chance at taking a breath was zero, and that was selfishly made known by the deep.

Finally, Joel gained his composure in the water. He noticed silence filling up all around him. It bound all through the deep, like horses jumping hurdles, never halting. The black was endless, not a floating particle of the sea was visible. In Joel's mind, he was drowning. He stopped fighting his freedom and instantly released his muscles against the resistance of the water and drifted freely, disappearing in blackness.

Seconds turned into minutes as Joel waited for death. Unaware of his breathing, his blue marble eyes pierced the dark, gazing afar, only to see solid emptiness hovering around his lifeless body.

He made an intensifying gasp, then another, and another. In his mind, he exhaled the notion of relief. "I'm alive, I'm alive!"

Instantly looking from left to right, trying to keep his balance at the same time, he gripped his face to feel a sensation of life. Suddenly, there was a grinding rumble of thunder and sparkles of lightning and gamma-rays, ferociously stabbing the water around him. The water split, as though a comb parted hair straight down the middle, stirring the deep with a throbbing intonation of current.

Joel's body was dropping downward even more, knocking out all the wind he had. Slowly, the storm ceased. Joel came alive again. Slithering shadows gracefully merged out of the walls of blackness. He stopped treading and kicking his feet, never taking his eyes off the vague shadows coming towards him. Startled, he blinked his eyes continuously to make sure that what he saw was real and not just a figment of his imagination. Joel's gifted sensitive hearing capability picked up remote voices. Scared to death, he attempted to swim upward again. The ghostly shadows of darkness came after him. Like magnets, they guided him back down, further than before. Than the vision of a ghost spoke, "Come."

"What do you want?" Joel thought angrily, while struggling to free himself. Terrified, he didn't realize that every thought and emotion was heard and understood by the long, shadowy image of the black sea. "Where are you taking me?" Petrified, he vigorously twisted and turned his body like a wet towel being rung out. He broke away from the frightful, hollow reflection that had forced him into a sphere that was not of this world.

Floating alongside the deep barriers, Joel felt a matter of energy gathering all around him. A soft accent with refinement spoke, "Leave from here...now." All at once, the wall of the deep opened to a whirling funnel of white light. Joel eyeballed the direction of the intense light and peered again at this unidentified black man unknown to him. Shockingly, his great grandfather and great uncle Seth were there too.

JAMES PAID HIS DEBT

The General Store made town folks come out. It was a gathering place for men to discuss business and women to meet other women's acquaintances. Children without any adults were the least likeliest to be seen around ol' man Creech's General Store, for he threatened them by shooting a gun up in the air. A youthful face was a thief, according to him.

James rode his wagon up to the front of the General Store and tied the horse up around the water well. As soon as he walked up to the step of the doorway, ol' man Creech, a tall slim, pale man with holes in his skin, greeted him with a sneered smile. His teeth were discolored russet with grimy yellow stains from chewing tobacco over time.

"Sa' dare, nah James, what's go'on?"

"Ah'd come by tuh make mah last payment."

"Comin." Ol' man Creech threw his arms around James, greeting him like they've been good buddies for years.

Before James walked in the store, he looked up to the faded blue sky, "Ah smell a storm comin' dis way."

"It's comin' dis evenin', so we'd betta take care of dis here business." He escorted James to the back of the store, entering ol' man Creech's private back room. As ol' man Creech turned the light switch on, he pulled out a chair for James to sit in. He sat behind his scruffy wooden desk and took out two dusty shot glasses from the drawer and started to pour a half empty bottle of whisky.

"Mista Creech, Ah'd wanna thankya fuh'ya kindness and not speakin' a word 'bout dis here transaction."

"Our pride is all we got...Rosa Lee can 'preciate a man lak yo'self."

"Well, here ya go Mista Creech."

"James, you can call me Adam, jis' plain ol' Adam, any man dat pays his debt on time and pays in full – can call me by mah first name."

Seth, ol' man Creech's son, storms in at the exchange of money.

"Ah'm all paid up," James said.

"Thankya kindly," ol' man Creech replied.

"Mah deed."

"Oh yeah, dat's right," said ol' man Creech, snapping his finger. He started looking, shuffling papers on his desk and then in his drawers.

"Gad Nabbit, wehs mah folder?" Slamming the drawers.

"Pa, you took a heap of papers home last night."

"Dat's right...Dese youngans are good fuh somthin'."

A strange thought had come to James for a second, but a thought that had disappeared in the creases of his facial expression.

"Well, you can still giv'mah the receipt, cantcha?"

"Ah'll pick up de deed soon after dinner dis evenin' and drop off t'yuh."

"Yuh sure?"

"Yas'im sure." Ol' man Creech grinning.

Ole man Creech wrote out the receipt and wrote in large letters at the bottom 'Paid In Full' along with his signature.

As James watched the handwriting of the receipt, he outlined his overalls straps with the back of his thumbs, inhaling and exhaling the mildewed-scented sacks of grain and the thin saw dust scattered across the floor of the dingy stock room. He slanted his cap forward and gallantly walked to the doorway of ol' man Creech's secretive back room, looking back at the old man, "I see 'ya lader dis evenin'." James walked out the door with the pride that goes with paying off a large debt. Relief!

"Sure thing," he mumbled while the corner of his mouth was twitching tobacco, rolling his tongue from side to side. Ol' man Creech sluggishly escorted James out the store. Almost in a nonchalant way, he shoved the door open for James, and before James could walk out the door, ol' man Creech spitted out a rotten

gruesome lewi across the front porch of the store.

Before leaving the store, James stopped in his tracks and stared up at the already-transformed clouds. "We 'bout to get dat storm. Looks like a heavy one."

The storm was about to set off howling winds. Thunder roared then the sky turned over to its darkest side. As James rode off in his buggy, ol' man Creech snorted, "Dat's one cullud dat pays his debt on time."

Gabe is standing next to him. "Pa, whatcha talkin' 'bout?"

"Nothin, nah grab a sack of dat meal and do some work 'round here!"

On the edge of the dock, Joel regained consciousness, with tears spilling all over his body. His eyes glued, he was curled up in a fetal position, holding his knees in his chest, weeping for desperation. "What do you want? What do you want?" he hollered out. Joel's anxiety was getting the best of him. The realization of his fretful encounter hinged on his soul like a hefty fisherman's hook being jabbed in his gut.

In the distance, footsteps swiftly moved through the pasture—the steps were heavy footprints meeting the grass, getting louder as the footsteps pummeled on the rigid planks of wood, one after the other in a hurry, and getting closer.

"You all right?" A voice shouted over Joel's loud whimpering.

It was Ned.

Joel moved restlessly, shifting position in an effort to prepare for his rescue. Ned grabbed him by the upper arms, his grip was urgent and warm.

"I don't know what happened." Joel grasping for breath.

Ned not saying a word continued to walk Joel home.

Nine

The night air blew calmly that evening, and the scattering leaves shoved each other on the ground. Holly knuckled her hands in the front pockets of her windbreaker and stood outside on the porch, waiting for peace to come over. She stepped off the ancient steps and started to walk, not really knowing where she was going. She noticed a fire burning from a distance and inquisitively, she swiftly moved closer. Holly crept closer and closer, halting at a strange finding. She saw her neighbor, sitting inside a circle formed by barrels of fire.

The neighbor sat motionless with his eyes outlining the different imprints on the sand that was made from stone pebbles and seaweeds washed ashore. A gruff, hoarse tone of voice spoke as though it were, for the first time, speaking. "Ah's know yo're dare, com'on out."

"What?" Holly very calmly said. She panicked and looked around the bushes with guilt.

"Ah ain't goin' tuh eat yuh," the elderly voice said.

"Excuse me."

"Naw, you have tuh ex'cuze me, Ah'm 80-years-old. Ah try tuh use mah sense of humor, or at least whut's left of it."

"Why are you sitting in the middle of fire?"

"It keeps me comp'ny when Ah run out'uh booze...you got some?"

"Let me guess, you're using your sense of humor again."

"Ah ain't playin' nah."

Holly stared at him with the utmost sincerity and looked from side to side, still not sure if this old man was alone. "Let me introduce myself. My name is Holly."

"Hah's yo' husband?"

Amazed and startled at his prompt question about Joel, not knowing about Joel's encounter with the deep, she answered warily. "That gentleman will soon be my husband and his name is Joel."

"You not legal?"

She looked at him with contempt, and the old man started to laugh through his cough.

"Don't choke," Holly said sarcastically.

"Folks call me Ned."

Holly looked around in the night air to get a feel for why Ned was really sitting in the middle of barrels lit with fire, but nothing came to mind. She stared at his surroundings, then smiled at him with sincerity, expecting the old man was just that, an old man. Ned was built square in the shoulders and wide across the chest. Holly could tell that he was a tall man, because the end of his knees extended far away from his crotch. Ned slightly lifted his head and made eye contact. "Mah fire isn't d'sturbin you?"

"No," Holly said.

Ned turned his head to the sounds of the waves. Holly followed his eyes, looking out into the descending deep.

"So, I understand you're the oldest native around Beaufort?" Holly asks, breaking up the moment of silence.

"Dares a few more of us left."

"Would you like to come over for dinner?"

Ned chuckled. "You mean sit wid you and yo' soon t'be husband at yo' dinner table?"

"Why yes," Holly said, ignoring his cunning remark.

"Ain't never ate wid white folks befo' – ate 'round dem and served dem, but ain't never broke bread wid dem."

Puzzlement came over Holly's face. "Well we are both in for a treat."

Ned laughed. "It's yo' first time too."

"No, this will be my first dinner in our new home."

"Hah'd you like yo' new home?"

"It's beautiful."

"Hah's yo' husband doin'?"

Holly instantly paused and a look of confusion came over her face. "He's fine," Holly replied slowly. "Since you are so interested in Joel, come over tomorrow night for dinner and you can ask him yourself."

"Ah thankya fuh de invitation but Ah can't promise yuh Ah'll be dere."

Holly entered the unpacked bedroom, searching for Joel. She pushed open the bathroom door and saw his silhouette through the clear shower curtains. Holly peacefully leaned against the bathroom doorway and interviewed each part of his body.

"Holly, is that you?" Joel opened the shower door and reached for the towel off the towel rack.

"Yes."

Joel walked over to Holly and opened his towel to include her. "Holly, I'm so sorry." Holly covered Joel's mouth with her index finger, not giving him a chance to disclose his second terrifying ordeal at the dock. He didn't want to anyway, so he kept quiet and let the words of forgiveness roll off his tongue. "It's over, let's go out tonight."

Holly hugged Joel and noticed a bruise on his upper arm. "What's that?"

"Nothing...I was unpacking and moving furniture today...I probably hit my arm, that's all." The truth was pain throbbed in his arm, but that hurt wasn't as much as the painful thought of losing Holly.

Ten

Moisture from the light rain fell on every tree branch and covered the sand along the shoreline. Holly and Joel decided to drive to town to meet Adrian and Carmen for dinner. Holly slid back in the seat of the car, shrugged her shoulders and shook off the tension. She noticed Ned eyeballing them, so Holly acknowledged his stare. It seemed like he obviously was nosy, but innocence disguised the curious creases on his face.

By this time, Joel was starting up the car. "What do you think he wants?" Joel rolled his window down and poked his head out the window. "Can we help you with something?"

Ned turned away at the sound of Joel's voice. It was as though Ned hadn't noticed Joel at all. Deep down, Joel wasn't eager to face Ned, for he was still shameful about his odious episode on the dock.

"Now what is his problem?" Holly asked, offended. "I know he saw me waving at him."

The evening moved forward and the light from the stars came shining through the night, lighting up the roads. The wind pushed the waves wildly to the shore. Without being near the ocean, there was no end to the brackish aroma. Seagulls flocked the ocean top for visible fish, calling out their sounds of hunger.

Closer to Beaufort's historical downtown, the lights got brighter while the streets got nosier. People from all walks of life, not sparing a moment of loneliness, filled the air on the busy sidewalks, shaped by old red brick stones leading miles of road. You saw many buildings covered with score plaster to resemble stone. Some of these buildings were utilized during the Civil War, are now churches. Homes that were build as early as 1844 became museums.

On their way back home from the restaurant, Joel and Holly harmonized to old school songs playing on the car radio. They had sung, "When a man loves a woman...Can't keep his mind on nothing else..."

Everything seemed to be fine. Holly snuggled close to Joel, smiling and grinning like a little girl that just received the best birthday gift ever. She was ecstatic over their dinner with Adrian and Carmen.

All of a sudden, the car's interior lights and headlights went out, and the yellow lines on the road were the only visible things to be seen. Holly sat up straight and looked around, startled.

"Honey, please tell me the car didn't stop."

"Okay, the car didn't stop."

"Joel, we are in the middle of nowhere, it's night, so please act concerned!"

Joel attempted to start the ignition. *Nothing.* He rambled in the glove compartment for the flashlight, hurried out of the car to inspect under the hood. As he bent over to investigate, he thought he heard something. He stood up and looked around, waiting for his ears to detect the sound again, but it was only silence drifting. Ignoring his first thought, he started back, looking under the hood. Joel heard it again. This time, he paced away from the hood of the car, walked towards Holly to see if she heard anything.

As they made eye contact, Holly rushed to roll down the window. "Honey, what's wrong?"

"Do you hear something?"

"Yeah, I don't hear the car running," she said jokingly.

"No, I'm serious," Joel said.

The crows came closer and called out to others. From above in the trees, they began to surround Joel and Holly.

"There you go, all you hear are crows. Now please, let's get going."

Joel and Holly smiled at each other with assurance and excused fear for that brief moment. Joel strolled to the front of the car to continue to look under the hood. Then Joel heard it again. Like an electric sound-wave under the sea, the whales were responding noisily. The infuriating sound kept getting louder and louder. Joel put his hands over his ears, turning around and around in circles.

Holly leaned towards the car window, looking shocked and frightened. Her hands dashed to open the car door, but it wouldn't open. She hammered the window to get Joel's attention, but the earsplitting sound continued to grow louder. Holly leapt to the driver's side to open the door but it wouldn't open. She jumped in the back and hysterically tried to open the back doors, but there was no way out. She tried to push buttons to let the windows down. Holly wasn't able to get to Joel; the feeling of helplessness overcame her as she sat watching the man she loved in trouble once again. Holly screamingly knocked on the window with her fists until bruised. Pleading. "God, please help me...please...please help me!"

The dead leaves tousled around Joel's feet as though they were performing a miniature tornado. Joel passed out and fell to the ground. The crows disappeared in the sky. The daunting droning sound of the crying whales was gone too.

Minutes later, Joel sluggishly sat up and held his head in his hands. He pulled himself off the cold pavement and scouted around to find Holly.

"Holly!" Shouted Joel. Still Holly could barely hear him. Joel stumbled towards Holly, calling her name. He approached the passenger side car window where Holly was sitting and saw Holly sitting as though nothing happened. Holly never looked his way. He looked up and glanced around the car and then back at Holly, looking over to the driver side, and gawked with amazement. The sight ripped Joel's eyes open.

An image was staring into Joel's eyes. Joel furiously tapped the window with his flashlight to get Holly's attention. Holly gazed intently out the front window, frozen. The night air grew cooler whereas the waves forcefully smacked the rocks. The cursing wind whipped the aged trees parallel to the road.

"Get the hell out of my car!" Bellowed Joel.

Instantly, Joel was thrown down on the side of the road. Trying to pull himself to his feet, he heard the car engine rumble. Scared out of his wits, he fell back down on the ground then rushed up the bank, reaching his hand out, pleading to stop.

"What do you want!"

Joel quickly ran to the car. Madly, he started to hit the driver side window with his flashlight.

"Who are you and what do you want?" Joel demanded.

Out of breath, wet hair clinging to his forehead, Joel looked directly into the car, the manifest stature was gone. He lifted the car door handle, and surprisingly, a clicking sound was a sigh of relief.

"Honey, what's wrong?" Holly looked at Joel – as nothing happened.

"Who the hell was that?" Joel yelled at Holly.

"Who?"

"That girl!"

"What girl?" Confused, Holly started observing outside the car.

"You mean to tell me that you didn't see that girl sitting in this car beside you?"

"No!"

"You lie!" Joel said. "Holly, I don't know what you're trying to pull, but it's not going to work."

Stunned, Holly got out of the car and asked Joel, "What girl are you talking about?"

"Two seconds ago, there was a black girl sitting in this car beside you."

"This man has lost his fucking mind," whispered Holly. "Okay Joel, a black girl was in the car, she spoofed you and disappeared. Now, can we please go home?"

"I'm not going anywhere with you until you tell me who? What? Where the girl went?"

"Joel," pleaded Holly, "I don't know who or what you saw, but can we please get back in the car and talk about this on the way home."

Silence. Joel did everything he could do to hold onto the piece of his mind that had escaped him a few minutes ago.

Joel walked back to the rear of the car and opened the trunk. He slammed it shut and slowly walked around to Holly with one arm behind his back with a baseball bat and the other arm down at his side.

"You drive."

"What are you going to do, beat the hell out of me and throw me on the side of the road?"

"No, I'm going to beat the hell out of you if you touch me."

"Joel, you're crazy, you know that!" Holly cried, feeling as if her head was about to explode.

"You either stay out here, or drive...make up your mind!" Joel commanded.

"Damn you, Joel!" Holly dashed over to the driver's side to get in the car while Joel agitatedly sat on the passenger side. He placed the baseball bat across his lap, gripping and caressing the handle for security.

Punching the gas for all she was worth, Holly drove like a bat out of hell. The tires bit into the gravel of the road, at the same time, as she braked at the stop light she kept her focus on Joel. Looking forward frantically then to the right, then straight ahead, then to the left, and the right again. Holly couldn't help but feel Joel was going to use that bat.

Back home, Joel's face was balmy red. He was breathing heavily, sitting stiffly in the living room, clutching the baseball bat that was still stretched across his lap, tapping his hands against it. Locked in the master bathroom, Holly sat on the edge of the tub, sobbing and cursing the evening, shedding tears of fear. Silence spread throughout the white cracked ceilings, down to the dusty crawl space surrounded by the land that once held a homemade wood and tin long ago. Lights throughout the house weren't spared, and this time, the outside breeze wasn't able to meet inside the windows. Joel never took his eyes off the doorway to the living room.

The doorbell rang. Holly steadily wiped her tears from her swollen eyes to listen for any movement or sound, thinking Joel might get the door since he was closest. The doorbell rang again. Holly lifted her head towards the bathroom wall with a loud sigh, "Good grief, are you going to answer the door?"

Holly stood in front of the mirror, holding her cheeks for relief and trying to figure out whether or not Joel was going to lose it again if she answered the door.

She summoned her courage and walked out the bathroom and down the hall. She passed Joel and answered the door.

"Whazzz up!"

A wounded face looked beyond Adrian and Carmen, then drifted downward and said, "Come in." Adrian and Carmen quickly transitioned from their exuberant stopover to a regretful visit.

"Holly, are you okay?" Softly asks Adrian.

Tearfully, she lifted her face upward to reach Adrian's anxious eyes and said, "No, I'm not okay."

Carmen scuttled closer to embrace Holly and Holly, for that instant, felt some of her damaged feelings recovered. "Holly, what's going on?"

Holly squeezed Carmen even tighter and cried, "Joel's gone crazy."

Adrian glanced around the dimly lit, half-empty house and asked, "Where's Joel?" Holly couldn't stop crying long enough to answer Adrian, so Adrian slowly crept around the house, obviously unaware of what he was going to find.

There was only one main light on in the house, and that was in the hallway at the front door. The reflection from the outdoor night-lights pierced through the windows throughout the house. Adrian spotted a dark shadow in the living room.

"Hey, Joel!"

Joel sat there, motionless and without saying a word.

Adrian felt more even compelled to get Joel to speak. "Man, we had a good time at dinner. Carmen really enjoyed herself and she adores Holly. We wanted to surprise you and Holly tonight with more champagne and bless the house. Not to mention, we are staying in Beaufort this weekend to help you guys unpack."

Silence followed.

"Joel, did you hear me? Say something, man."

Slowly, Joel pulled the brass string of beads down from the colorful lamp shade that was adjacent to the brown leather chair he was occupying. Sweat dripped sporadically and blood vessels heated his face like a glass sitting in the sun. Adrian, speechless at first, backed up and studied Joel's stiff body language and realized he was holding a baseball bat.

"Joel, man, what's going on?"

"Adrian, that bitch is trying to kill me off." Joel said, tearing up with panic.

"Who?" Adrian was shocked, opening his eyes wide and looking around the grim room with apprehension, steadily distancing himself from Joel.

"She couldn't even wait until we got married."

"Holly?"

"Who else!"

"Joel, do you know what you're saying?"

"Adrian, look at me," Joel pleaded. "I'm holding a bat, for Christ sake, and Holly is trying to hurt me and I'm going to do something that I'm going to regret the rest of my life."

Adrian desperately wanted to know what was going on between Holly and Joel. He begged Joel tell him what happened, and wanted him to start at the beginning. Adrian assured Joel everything was going to be okay and slowly retrieved the bat out of Joel's hands.

"I'm not going to let Holly hurt you. Let's put this bat away, go in the kitchen, and have a cup of coffee."

Joel collapsed into the palms of his hands as Adrian helped him to his feet. Joel and Adrian walked into the kitchen. Holly and Carmen were already seated at the round wooden table. At first, quietness filled the small kitchen, and then squeals from the chairs being moved out from the table were the only sounds to be heard.

"Joel and Holly, I don't know what's going on, but we are going to get to the bottom of this. I've known you guys for a long time. You're like my big brother and sister. I want to help."

Carmen patiently waited for Adrian to finish consoling Joel and Holly. "Can we turn on some lights? I think if we see each other real good, we can talk to each other openly." As Carmen went to turn the switch on in the kitchen, the doorbell rang. Carmen looked to Joel and Holly to get permission to answer the door.

Then Carmen swiftly walked down the hall and noticed a picture on the wall. She marched up to the picture with a smile, outlining the cracked wooden frame with her skinny fingertip. Then her eyes rested in the middle of the dusty glass. Her sudden discovery had her smiling until she answered the door, "Who is it?"

The moon was full then the breeze left a chill spell outside. It was Ned, standing there with his old over-worn, washed, blue overalls and a beat up faded baseball cap. Carmen cracked the door just enough to see the dark, tall figure standing before her.

"Hello."

"Good evenin', ma'am. Ah'm Mista Joel's neighbor. I was passin' by and wanted to check in on him and de miss'."

"Oh," Carmen paused to think. "Can you come back another time?"

"Well, Ms. Holly invited me to dinner."

"Tonight!" Startled

"Yesim."

"But it's late."

"Well, Ah reckon so. Ah was never good at tellin' time."

She stared at him for a bit and noticed the numerous wrinkles, white-silver hair and tired face standing before her.

"Hi, I'm Carmen and you are?"

"Ned, pleased tuh meet yuh."

"That's an easy name to remember," Carmen said, smiling.

"Well, Ah's betta be on mah way."

"Ned, please come back tomorrow. Right now, it's not a good time. I'm sure they will love to have you over," Carmen pleaded.

"You think Ah can talk to Mista Joel right quick?"

"Joel is not in any condition to talk to anyone right now."

"He's not feelin' good?" Ned suspiciously probed.

"Trust me, good is not the word, if you know what I mean."

Ned turned around to look up at the sky. Hesitantly, he wanted to say something, but caught his tongue and turned back to face Carmen. "Thank ya, ma'am."

Carmen shut the door, and Ned turned back around slowly on the porch and gazed at the black sea as though he was praying silently. The sound of the waves slapping the rocks played an angry symphony. The moon lit up the ground just enough to create a luminous path on the land to see Ned home. Blackbirds mobbed the sky, soaring through the mystifying air above the sea orchestra. They gathered one by one on the mended old dock.

Eleven

Silence flowed all through the cracked, painted white house, carrying a mild-scented seaweed breeze - just enough to inhale without squinting your face. The off-white sheer curtains blew uninterrupted, allowing solace to settle in the evening atmosphere. Under the stars, the breath of the bustling breeze stirred the mysterious ocean and lulled over a vista from miles away, as though the restored house was floating in a picture.

An unexplained past was buried underneath the land and throughout the house. Oblivious of its mystifying influences, it was about to launch its intentions on Joel and on others who shared his company.

Adrian and Carmen decided to sleep over that night following the round table chat in the kitchen. Holly and Carmen slept in the bedroom while Joel and Adrian slept in the living room area adjacent to the front door. Everyone was sound asleep except Joel.

Joel's restless body haunted him with guilt for Holly. He gazed at the ceiling, looking for serenity, hoping that it came before daybreak. He rolled over on his side to lift the bat up from the floor and stared at it with regret. Slowly he eased himself up into a sitting position, groaned and smacked his forehead. He threw the bat down on the sofa with regret and asked himself, "How could I have been so stupid. What's wrong with me?" Joel's guilt lifted him from the sofa and guided him down the hallway's hardwood floors to Holly.

Silently, he stepped into the bedroom. The walls were covered with beige-striped wallpaper. A round antique oriental rug covered the middle of the floor. The bed, nightstand, wicker chair, and the old dresser that came with the house were the only furnishings in the room. Joel felt like a fool as he stared at Holly sleeping calmly.

He eased himself down on the edge of the bed beside Holly and slowly reached out to stroke her cheeks, but quickly slapped his arm back.

Quietly, Holly moaned, sensing his presence. "You're not going to hurt me, are you?"

Joel whispered earnestly, "I'm so sorry, Holly."

Holly quickly propped herself up, stripping away the sheet from her upper body, and lunged herself into Joel's arms.

Carmen woke, scratching her butt. "Thank goodness. Now I can sleep with my man." Carmen swiftly tip-toed around the bed, embracing Joel and Holly. "I love you guys." She dashed out the bedroom door as though Adrian was waiting for her with open arms.

"You know what? We have the best friends."

"I know," Joel softly said. He inhaled and blew out of his mouth, then made a heart wrenching face and squeezed Holly's hands for assurance as he continued to express his deepest apologies.

Holly looked up at him as though she were enjoying a proud moment from him to remember forever. "Are you finished?"

"Yes."

"Now come to bed and keep me warm," Holly said softly.

Hours later - a rancid stench entered the room and awakened Joel. He sat straight up in bed, sniffing continuously and looking around the room. He pulled the sheets off Holly to see if she was the cause, or if she noticed the unbearable odor. Holly was sound asleep, so he gently swooshed the sheets back onto her body. Joel slid off the edge of the bed.

His feet stepped into freezing black water, ankle high, surrounding the bedroom. Joel mentally collapsed with panic, reaching out to Holly, shouting her name. Nonetheless, not a sound was to be heard in return. The ice-cold black water immobilized Joel's legs and muted his voice.

"Holly, wake up, wake up!" Joel desperately shouted. Joel's eyes urgently worked the bedroom for anything that would help him, but to his horrifying astonishment, the water was rising up to his hips and Holly was under water. "Dear God! Please help me!" There was nothing Joel could do to save Holly. "Holly, wake up! Holly wake up!" Joel viciously screamed.

Holly never moved out of her arched position. Again and again, he screamed out for Holly.

"Holly wake up, wake up," a childish voice mimicked.

Joel immediately held still, like radar picking up radio sound waves at an unvarying speed. He slowly turned his head away from the bed, closed his eyes and opened them back up again, staring motionless and speechless, he cried miserably. "What do you want?"

The bleak arctic murky water started rising once more. By this time, it was at Joel's chest. "I'll do anything you want. Please don't do this!" Horrified.

The sight paralyzed Joel's soul, enabling him to catch enough breaths to comprehend what was before him; he realized he was the only one that could see her. Her eyes were completely dark brown and shiny, there were no whites to her eyes. She wore a yellow and blue plaid skirt, knee-length, above her white-laced trimmed ankle socks. A perfect pink ribbon gave notice to her presence.

"You were in the car that night with Holly," said Joel shivering. The room lit up like a storm of the century. "You're not fucking real; this is some sick dream!"

The misty water began to rise again, only this time, boiling then turning bloody.

Struggling to push himself away from the figure that laughed at him, he rapidly shook his head and wiped the foul water away from his face. Then he thrust his arms out, pointing and shouting, "You're nothing but a dream! You hear me, you're nothing but a dream!"

White electric rays vaulted the ceiling, diametrically clashing with the bedroom, striking framed pictures on the walls, sweltering–lightning struck continuously and it wasn't going to stop anytime soon. The ripping sound went on and on the further he sunk. Joel lost his hearing.

DEEP SLEEP

Despairingly flapping his arms and feet, Joel continued to go down into the ocean's abyss. The bedroom's formation faded away then the black became visible, as though it were there all the time. Mouth and eyes locked opened, Joel floated upright, paralyzed, dead-looking and barely breathing. Yet again, the deep's wall opened another chronicle.

GABE AND SETH

Gabe and Seth strolled the simmering dust roads till dusk each day. It was likely to find them stirring up trouble and terrorizing the nearby school kids. They didn't attend school, except when they felt like it. Even ol' man Creech didn't make them go to school. He believed in working Gabe and Seth as needed and thought school was a waste of time.

On this day, they loafed around until they came upon the house where Ned once resided. Some of the homes on the island spread across its shoulder between six and ten acres apart; they were built far enough away from each other to know trespassing wasn't going to be an issue. Gabe and Seth weren't surprised to see the empty house. Jokingly, they staked their claim on it, not knowing the home's destiny.

As they returned home that day, they came across their father working on a horse wagon. Seth kept walking and Gabe slowed down. Just the fear alone of passing ol' man Creech made Gabe nervous.

"Boy, fetch me dem nails 'round yonder," he said, slothfully chewing tobacco, then spitting it out with no sense of direction, nearly missing Gabe's filthy beat-up shoes. Gabe didn't dare talk back to ol' man Creech. Ole man Creech was the kind of man you didn't cross inside or outside of the home – son or no son.

"Damn boy, can't yuh hear?"

"Yesim." Gabe said startled. Gabe ran to the back of the barn to fetch the nails. He came upon Seth bent down on his knees in the back of the barn.

"Whatcha lookin' at?"

Seth had discovered their Pa's secret burial ground. This was where ol' man Creech stored his money, valuables, and other things that didn't rightfully belong to him, in an old cigar box buried underground in the back of the barn. The only reason why Seth came upon it was that he himself was searching for a secret place to bury his stolen things.

"Pa's gonna whip you silly!" Gabe said, scared to death.

"Shut up and stop bein' uh whissy!"

"Seth, Pa is goin' tuh shoot you dead, good as Ah'm standin' here." Gabe said, shaking but curious himself.

"Gabe, look at dis stuff...yur still wearin' shoes wid holes and Ah keep patchin' up these same ole overalls...look at all dis money!"

"I don't know, Seth, please put de box back," he said, panicking.

"Look at all dese papers." Curiously, he tried to read each piece of paper. "Dey look official...Lak some kind of 'mportant papers." They were land plats and deeds.

Gabe snatched them out of Seth's hands and read some of them out loud, studying the words printed on the deed. *"Look at dis; he's got Ned's Pa deed...but why?"*

Seth snatched back the papers and threw them back down in the box and said, *"Nah we know why de house was empty."*

"Hey, Seth pass me dat watch."

"Hey, Ah'd remember dis watch. D'is Mista Willsworth's watch. Pa promise tuh give dis back tuh'um when he gave'um de money fo' de lumber to bury his wife...Ah know because I wuz dare when Mista Willsworth paid Pa back." Seth looked confused, tossing the broach in the palm of his hand. *"Nah Ah's know why Mista Willsworth kept comin' tuh de store arguin' wid Pa...Well hell, he's dead nah."*

Gabe heard a noise and quickly turned his head towards the barn door, looking beyond the entry of the barn. *"Shhh!"* For a split second, he heard steps on foot from afar and quickly hid behind the heavy square bundles of hay stacks. Seth froze and silence was captured as though a grasshopper was being caught and sealed in a jar. A slim grey cat jumped

73

off the seat of the tractor-trailer. It swiftly ran over the scattered hay that was spread across the barn, out to the sun.

"Damn you Gabe, git!"

Gabe clumsily ran to the work table in the barn, grabbed the nail box, and ran out. Unexpectedly, Ole man Creech turned the corner of the barn and Gabe's breath was snatched away as he fell to the ground.

"Boy, what de hell takon yuh so long?"

Gabe held his right hand over his chest to calm his heart beating and held out the box of nails, spitting out dust stirred up from his fall. "Pa Ah'got dem nails, see."

Ole man Creech snatched the nail box out of Gabe's hand, "Good fo' nothin." Then he walked away.

The moment of rationality was instant – Joel raised his head up and started to decline further down into the unknown black water. Mysteriously, a bright white gradient light halted and shielded Joel's lifeless body, slowly guiding him to the top. Joel was soaked plus reeked a strong odor of Beaufort's Atlantic elements.

Comatose and surrounded by miry puddles in the destroyed bedroom, skin bloodless, with spider web eyes, he exhaustingly inhaled short breaths then exhaled one right after the other. Slowly but surely, he found the strength to take a deep breath and started to cough. After each cough, he continuously wiped off the dripping thick foam hanging from his mouth. The last cough was so hard, he threw up the murky black water that came from another world. As the coughing ceased, he struggled with himself on the hardwood floor that seeped puddles between its hidden cracks. Shockingly, he realized he was back in the bedroom.

With all his strength, he peeled his body off the floor. He stretched his right arm straight up, gripping the aged dresser attached to a thick, mahogany-framed mirror, and pulled his body up to a standing position. Firmly pressing down on the dresser top with both hands to hold up his body weight, he slowly lifted has face, only to stare at the horror that engaged his soul and immobilized him. The mirror reflected a message smeared in greenish-blue muck from the ocean's belly: *She's in the house.*

Joel stepped back from the mirror, terrified and eyes full of fear. "My God! What do you want from me?" Joel cried as he bent forward, clutching his fists with fury. *Silence.*

Little by little, he lifted his head to stare back at the mirror. He saw Holly through the reflection of the mirror, still in the bed as though she were untouched.

"Holly, Holly," he tearfully tried to get his voice past the saliva caught in his throat. "Holly, we have to go." He firmly shoved her shoulders. "Holly wake up now, we have to get out of here!" He hysterically shook her shoulder.

Holly's eyes flew open from the forceful shake. She stared at Joel as though she didn't know him anymore. "Joel, what the hell happened to you?"

"Holly, we can't talk now. We have to go, please, let's leave this house, now!"

Holly steadily inspected Joel's tormented, dripping wet body and knew his soul was bruised. Something was wrong. Without hesitating, she quickly turned her head and looked around the bedroom. Completely stunned, she hastily tore the sheets away from her body and jumped out of bed. She cuffed her hand over her mouth, puking from the stench and the disastrous piles of debris left behind from a mysterious malevolence that had something to do with Joel. Joel walked near Holly to try to console her. Holly threw her arm out, holding the palm of her right hand up to Joel's face to stop him. "Get away from me!"

"Holly, I can't explain what happened, all I know is that we have to get out of here," he pleaded with Holly.

"You mean to tell me that this all happened while I was asleep!" Holly shrieked. "How come this room looks like it's been in a tornado and you along with it. I'm not wet. Can you explain that to me, Joel?"

Shaking his head and desperately crying, "Holly, please – we have to go!"

"I'm not going anywhere with you."

"Holly, take a good look at me and this room, do you think I can do something like this? You know me. I'm Joel...I would never do anything to hurt you or myself. All I know is that we have to get out of this house."

Holly, for a second, let her guard down and opened up to Joel. "Where's Adrian and Carmen?"

Joel's eyes filled with terror; his harrowing anticipation to get out the house just took a turn for the worse. "No!" Within seconds, Joel and Holly dashed out the bedroom towards where Adrian and Carmen were sleeping. As Joel was waking up Adrian and Carmen, Holly noticed the other parts of the house were intact.

Holly eagerly tried to get Joel's attention, "Look around you!" She turned around in a circle, holding out her arms.

"What are we looking at?" Adrian asked, sitting upright and wiping drool from his mouth, looking at Joel. Adrian's squinted eyes opened just enough to detect Joel's beat up and foul odor. "What the hell happened to you?"

"We don't have time to talk now. Get Carmen and let's get out of the house."

"Man, what's going on!"

"Someone's in the house," Joel aguishly said.

"Who's in the house?" Carmen squirmed into an upright position on the sofa. "It's cold in here," Carmen commented. As she laid eyes on Joel, she postured-up. "What happened to you?"

All of a sudden, the green glass lamp sitting on the end table by the window flew off with such force that it shattered against the wall.

Scared, Adrian said, "Did you see that shit?"

"Come on, baby. Let's get the hell out of here." Adrian and Carmen scrambled to get out of bed. Managing to group together, they scurried for the front door. Adrian turned the knob, but it wouldn't open. Suddenly, all the windows slammed shut in the house, leaving one entry open that led to the kitchen.

Heart pounding like a jackhammer, breathing as he had been running a marathon, Joel goggled Holly. "Do you think I'm crazy now?"

Holly was baffled with fear and ran to the phone at the foot of the stairs, across from the front door. "No dial tone." Holly tapped her cheek bones with her hands and wept out of desperation.

"What do you want?" Joel bellowed angrily, arms opened to the air.

"Joel, what does who want?" Holly said, with a draining voice, looking up from her sleek eyelashes. Everyone laid eyes on Joel, as if he were holding something back.

Within seconds, Joel cracked – instantly he was like a five-year-old tattle-tell boy, expressing grief, "I don't know who they are, and I think my great uncle knew them...and there's this little black girl that keeps hunting me and I don't know what she wants."

"Is it that black girl you saw in the car?" Holly asks.

"Yes," he shamefully said.

"What's that smell?" Adrian said, sniffing. "Well, let's not stick around and wait for it to bite us in the ass. Let's get out of this house then talk later."

Carmen grabbed the broken lamp off the floor, holding the broken base out in front of her like a knife and marched to the kitchen, murmuring, *"As I walk through the valley of death, I fear no evil, thy rod and thy staff they comfort me and will shield me all the days of my life...Thee that consumes evil in this house, your wickedness is misplaced and you will not drown us in your punishment. Leave from here now."*

Upon entering the kitchen, Carmen hesitantly pushed open the swinging door. Slowly, they crept into the kitchen. The appalling smell became even more unfathomable. "My Gawd! What is that smell?"

"It's death," Carmen replied. A sense of overwhelming danger was growing in Carmen - a feeling that someone was indeed upon them and wanted their attention. "Ya'll, there's a bad spirit in this house and we got to stay together."

Unexpectedly, there were thunderous vibrations rocking the house, as though it was being lifted from the center blocks and bricks. Holly's fearful eyes gazed at Joel.

By this time, Adrian was fed up and wanted out of the house. He picked up a kitchen chair and slammed it against the back door window. The glass shattered to smithereens, the shards vigorously blowing inward, piercing open Adrian's naked face and straight thru his clothed body.

Boisterous winds mixed with the echoes of galloping horses and wheels turning on wet gravel. The fierce winds made it impossible for them to come to Adrian's aid. Carmen fought the winds back, as though she had a score to settle, angrily shouting, "You have no place here! We've been dipped in the blood of righteousness, saved by our Lord Jesus Christ, you have no place here, you have no place here." She kept repeating faintly, 'you have no place here', dropping to her knees, uttering other words that only the supernatural tongue can speak.

Suddenly, the evil blizzard in the kitchen stopped. It was like someone turned down a dimmer switch on a wall, and everything turned off. Carmen scrambled and stumbled to her feet, beat up by the forceful winds, exhausted. "There's no evil here." She kicked the broken plates and pots from her path and made it to Adrian, quickly trying to stop his bleeding.

"Baby, what was that?" Adrian asked, never taking his eyes off Carmen's eyes as he lay in her arms.

"What was what?" Carmen asked.

"How did you know to say all that stuff to stop it?"

"I didn't, it just came to me. I guess the Holy Spirit protected us."

Adrian stared at Carmen, shaking.

"Don't worry honey, we're going home."

Deep down, Adrian knew there was something extraordinary about Carmen that was indescribable to the uninformed ordinary minds of some men. It was then that he made up his mind. Carmen wasn't just another woman who had the qualities of a 'Good Woman', but a woman who had an unknown passage among angels.

Shaken from the demonic ordeal that had stirred up every bodily fluid inside their bodies, Joel, Holly, Adrian and Carmen walked away from the kitchen towards the front door. As they moved down the hall, Carmen detected a discolored barrette matted in an old picture frame that was tilted on the wall. She glanced candidly, asking herself, "Why would anyone frame a barrette?"

Twelve

That same night the air was thick and humid—the heaven's drizzle blended in with the Atlantic. Ned emotionally sighed as he stared at the front door of the wooden house, set up on short columns of brick and cinder blocks, which was once his home. He stood straight up, not an arch in his back or legs, deep in thought and tremors in his heart, waiting for a movement from the ocean or a sign to come through the night.

JAMES'S 72 ACRES

James put up his land to build a home for his family. He went to ol' man Creech for the materials and money. In exchange, James's land was collateral. James signed the land over to ol' man Creech with an agreement to repay him every week until the debt was paid off and the land would go back to James and his family. He asked ol' man Creech to keep this agreement between them; he didn't want Rosa Lee to know that he put up the 72 acres to build the house. Before James's death, he made the last payment to ol' man Creech. James went to ol' man Creech's store and made his last payment, but ol' man Creech didn't have the deed at the time. Ol' man Creech made arrangements to meet James on that same evening to give the deed back to him. A death of a storm was brewing that same evening and James never made it home that night. Ole man Creech never turned over the land to James's family, for he knew Rosa Lee didn't know about the arrangement between James and him.

James hadn't been in the ground for nearly six hours before ol' man Creech came to Rosa Lee to inform her that James owed him a debt. He explained that James signed over the 72-acres of land as collateral to build the house, while waving the deed in her face at the same time. Devastated, Rosa Lee explained that she had no way to repay him at that time. Ole man Creech replied, "Right now, as it stands, dis here is my land and hause – you either pay off de debt yo' huzbun owes me or you git."

Soon after, Rosa Lee took on a journey to settle her scorned heart and to justify her husband's death. "He will not have died in vain fo' nothin'." She knew her husband worked hard for the family, and gave them a place of sanctuary with the essentials needed in life that some folks did not have and will never have. Rosa Lee also knew James always paid his debts and on time. The nervous tension in her gut sustained her feelings of suspiciousness, so she involved the law. When it came right down to it, the judge granted ol' man Creech the land – due to the fact the James had signed over the property to ol' man Creech as collateral in accordance with the agreement that he paid ole man Creech back in full. There was no evidence that James paid ol' man Creech in full; therefore, to the judge, James's debt had not been satisfactorily paid off. A verdict awarded ol' man Creech the 72 acres along with the house, as agreed by the deceased.

Within hours after the depraved verdict, Rosa Lee, Joseph and Lula moved in with Rosa Lee's parents across the way. Rosa Lee never told Joseph and Lula the truth about why they had to leave their home. It was as though infamy filled her like a tea bag in steamed water—not being able to hold onto the one-hundred-forty-year-old inheritance.

It hardened the blood in her veins and made living a droning task. Every now and then, the site of devotion stared into their faces remorselessly from a distance.

DEEP SLEEP

*Even though, Rosa Lee forbade
Joseph and Lula to step foot on that
land again, Lula simply refused to
comply. She continued to visit the
open water that rested underneath the
dock that had watched over her for
fourteen years. Nevertheless, the deep-
sea became Lula's diary and the
thought of not being able to share her
next chapter was unimaginable.*

*Another summer was conceded
and no one moved on the land or in
the house, and the folks around town
never questioned why – they knew ol'
man Creech was the root of James's
family losing their home, but not one
word was said about it.*

By this time, Ned was wet all over from the light
rain that sustained him willingly for whatever was
going to happen to him at that moment. He was getting
weary and his knees began to buckle. Trying to contain
himself, he pulled down the front of his navy blue,
worn-out baseball cap that had the letters "SC" stitched
on it, and stepped back, little by little. With his tired
eyes just about covered, he tucked his hands down into
the front pockets of his dingy overalls, then walked
away from the house that guarded the cavernous sea

border, which lined the shoulders of Beaufort, South Carolina. Midnight turned over to morning, but no indication of it could be felt or seen by the Atlantic.

Thirteen

Back in Atlanta, Adrian visited Carmen. For the first time, he walked through her door with the perception of an invite. Usually, he invited himself in. Standing still, he looked at the decorated windows with beige and brown curtains touching the polished wood floors. Every book, CD and magazine was categorized in the oak armoire. Carmen's apartment was spotless. Then he quietly sat down on the leather sofa, intently gazing at Carmen who was dancing from across the room.

Carmen was wearing headphones and bopping to music. She didn't notice Adrian's presence and kept boogying as though she were the lead singer and the only one on stage. She step danced across the floor, turning in circles, snapping and clapping, and singing out load. "Take your time...you can do it...take your time...that's right you can do it!" Sweat soaked thru her skin while beads of sweat assembled across her double-D cleavage.

Adrian lost himself in Carmen for that moment. For the first time in his life, he discovered true love, a calm soul that loves unconditionally, honestly and that was spiritually well-rounded. From a distance, in the living room, he focused on a beautiful sight that he thought no other man knew. A woman who had a special bond between earth and heaven, didn't fear evil itself, feared no form or shape, and could communicate with the unknown of this world. Adrian longingly stared and walked towards Carmen's workout. He stood at the doorway, both hands in his pocket, never blinking and attracting Carmen's eyes.

"Hey honey," said Carmen, out of breath.

Adrian smiled. He slowly walked closer and stood in front of her as she moved in place. "Hello, my angel."

"Baby, I'm working off all that Beaufort sea food we ate."

"You don't have to," Adrian said quietly.

"No way, baby...me and these thighs got to work out three times a week. I got to keep my pretty figure for my handsome man."

"I'm not afraid of a little weight."

"You say that now...!"

"Carmen, all I know is that I love you just the way you are and I want you in my life."

There was genuineness in his voice, though it had her to slow her exercising down.

Carmen felt something was wrong. "Adrian what's wrong with you?" she said, strangely looking at him.

"Carmen, what other woman can keep me pure? What other woman out there can hold my heart in place and know my every thought?" He clutched his hands as though he were about to pray. "You know, when something is troubling me, you know how I think, and you respect that, and you know when my heart is uneasy," Adrian softly said, deeply staring into Carmen's eyes. "When I can't use my hands, your hands become my hands. When I can't see, your eyes become my eyes. You've accepted me for me. You never asked me for anything that I couldn't give you."

"Baby, I keep you pure, because I'm pure. I didn't always know your heart, but I've learned your heart. Holly cupped Arian's right cheek with her hand. "You too, know when something is troubling me and know how I think. And I too, respect you for that."

"Carmen as you know, I am a child of God and I do believe in Him." Adrian said as though he was reassuring himself. "I have to admit, I've never seen His work." He had the grace to feel a little ashamed of himself.

"Yes you have, you just didn't know it. Your sight took over your faith."

"God is telling me something right now."

"What is it?" Even while she was holding his cheek, she still didn't let his eyes go.

"Before I came here, I read a passage in my bible and constantly went back to these verses. First Corinthians 11:7-8...but the woman is the glory of the man. For the man is not of the woman; but the woman of the man." Adrian gently pulled away Carmen's hand and tightly squeezed her hands in his. "Carmen you're my Glory." Locked in a stare, Adrian told her that he meant every word.

Carmen wiped the salty sweat off her forehead, and then turned the music off. "Honey, do I need to sit down?"

"No, but I need to kneel down."

Fourteen

In the city, the tree leaves are tainted gold, highlighted with orange. Some are garnished brown with red tones, lifeless. The dead leaves shuffle free on the aged and cracked sidewalks and wrestle on the streets as cars pass by.

Traffic was at a standstill and motorists were being attentive to others, weaving in and out of lanes on I-75 North. Joel and Holly swerved to the HOV lane of the four-lane expressway, to move with the continuing traffic. "Home-Sweet-Home!" Joel contentedly stated. Holly stared at her expression in the passenger side mirror, soothing her silver coffee traveling mug with her hands.

"Yeah, back to the hustle and bustle," smirked Holly.

"All I know is that I would rather be sane living with bumper to bumper traffic, than going out of my mind living in hell where there's no traffic. You feel me!"

Holly slouched forward, looking at the on-going traffic ahead of her, then turned her head towards Joel.

"I take it, you don't feel like talking about what happened in Beaufort?" Holly's voice was flat. Joel realized that Holly was talking while she was gawking out the window. All of a sudden, it was as though she was seeing a mysterious object in the sky for the first time. Her voice exploded. "Joel, I know you are going to get upset at me for saying this, but something was trying to get to you."

"What do you mean, me? What about you, Adrian and Carmen? We were all hunted!"

"Yes, Joel, we were all hunted but not toyed with like you – listen. The first night in the house, you had a dream that something was leading you out to the Atlantic Ocean. Three days later, you went to sleep and woke up out your mind." Joel nodded acknowledgement without meeting Holly's eyes. Then he decided to tell her what happened to him at the dock in Beaufort.

"Now, you're telling me, you were on the dock and almost drowned."

"I wasn't drowning. Something was pulling me under."

"Exactly!" Holly pointed her index finger up. "And what about the night the car stalled? Only you saw a girl sitting beside me."

"Oh, let's not forget about the two brothers." Joel said, getting upset.

Holly started to explain. "The night Adrian and Carmen stayed over...you fell into a deep sleep."

Joel hastily interrupted, "No Holly, that wasn't a deep sleep – that was under 100 feet of pure hell!"

"And you saw that girl again," Holly excitedly pointed out, as she put her coffee mug in the holder and began to express to Joel her thoughts. "Joel, do you realize when you were always around water, you were the only one that could see the girl. It seems to me that you and water have something in common – whatever that was back on that island, it wanted you badly."

"That's ridiculous. We've been back in Atlanta for almost three weeks now. I've never slept better. I swim every other day at the athletic club and I can swim all day. I get out of my bed – my feet land on hardwood floors, by the way."

"Joel, don't you get it. It was that house!"

"That's why we are here and that damn house is there." Joel snarled out loud and punched the steering wheel.

"But Joel…"

Joel threw her a quick look. "I don't want to talk about it, anymore!" Joel saw that they had reached the side street where the parking garage was located. He sped up, turning right into the parking facility and swerving into the space that was painted 165 in Arial yellow, bold letters.

Before Joel opened the car door, she could feel him facing her. "Look honey, I didn't mean to yell at you. I want to put this behind us, besides; no one is going to believe us. Let's be thankful we got our jobs back and we're living our lives again—Okay?"

Holly, zombified, scrolled through the office, keeping her mind refreshed of the conversation she had with Joel. Something was wrong. That was the firm conviction Holly couldn't get out of her mind. She started talking to herself. "That house is there and Joel is here…if Joel was there in the house, he would be sought after. As long as Joel is here, he's not hunted. What does Joel have to do with that house?" She uttered as she turned the knob into the employees' break room.

Adrian, energetically, walked in and noticed Holly pouring a cup of coffee. "Welcome back!"

"Good morning, Adrian. What's gotten into you?"

"I'm about to marry the most beautiful lady in the world!"

"Oh Adrian, I am so happy for you guys...what a minute, I'm her new best friend and she hasn't mentioned a thing to me."

"Don't worry, she will tonight."

"She doesn't know yet?" Holly stunningly asked.

"Tonight starts my journey to make Carmen the happiest woman in the world. I want to give her something her father didn't live long enough to give her. I want to give her something her mother can only dream of giving her."

"And what's that?"

"Me." Jokingly. "Seriously, happiness. I'm going to marry my queen in Cape Town, Africa!"

"That is going to be so beautiful. You two deserve it – you're both a good catch. If there is anything you need, let me know and don't be afraid to ask."

Adrian gently embraced Holly. As she cuffed her arms around him to congratulate him on his marriage proposal, she felt a sense of loneliness.

"Let's make it a double wedding." Adrian proposed.

"That would be great – the only problem is that your friend stopped talking marriage since we came back from Beaufort."

"Give him some time. He's probably still freaked out. I still am too for that matter. I mean, Holly...what we experienced in that house is what I watch on the chiller network or in the movies."

Holly changed the mood. She stepped back and quickly held her hand out. "You still owe me – I haven't forgotten you said a curse word in Beaufort."

"Oh, you didn't hear...this week's payroll checks bounced, hit me back next week." Jokingly.

Quarter past eight and silence settled in that same evening like dim lights diffusing in darkness, just enough to soothe the vision. Rain hit the large classic French windows in the living room. The room was decorated with earth tones and plush leather mahogany sofas. A half glass of red wine sat on the edge of the glass coffee table. Holly still agonized over her thoughtful discovery of the connection she made between Joel and water. The house that sat off the shoals of Beaufort was too great for her to ignore or take lightly, for that matter. Just thinking about the horror Joel experienced was enough for Holly to dig deeper.

"Why, why, why Joel?"

She tried to think, to sort things out, to strike out the confusion that was in her mind. But her thoughts raced and the images she needed to try to put any kind of coherent facts together melted away like sugar in a cup of coffee.

Given up for the moment, she took a sip of her wine, turned on the TV—it was tuned to the Discovery Channel. It was impossible. Holly's mind was in such turmoil that nothing said on TV registered.

"Dear God, I know I haven't followed You throughout my life, but I'm a good person. I want to know you. I'll learn. Please help me." She didn't know exactly what to say, or how to pray for it's been a long time. "Why Joel?" she softly asked herself again. Unexpectedly her body responded independently of her mind: Her breathing quickened; her heartbeat sped up; her muscles tensed.

"Yes." Holly jumped up and quickly rushed to the armoire. She pulled a dingy leather photo album out of the bottom drawer, flipping the pages. "I knew the scenery looked familiar to me." Holly looked up toward the ceiling, "Thank You."

Holly saw that the daunting house that she and Joel left behind was the exact house Joel's great grandfather & great uncle lived in – except that the house had somewhat been modernized. The house had been in Joel's family for over 60 years. In the faded black and white photo, there were two white boys, and in the background looking on was a black boy holding a shovel. The white house was cut off but sat off to the left side, silhouetted against the ocean on the torn-edged photo. Astonished, Holly rapidly turned to the other page of photos and realized there was one of Joel's relatives. She carefully pealed the aged photo from the book and placed it in her rich red alligator purse on top of the kitchen counter-top. Eagerly, she reached for the cordless phone.

"Hey...what's up?"

A scream came through the phone. "Girl I'm getting married!"

"I know, I know!" Holly said excitingly.

"What do you mean, you know?"

"Ahhh nothing. I mean, I know you are so happy and I'm so jealous of you."

"I love him, too." Carmen smiled.

"You want to take a ride with me to Beaufort?"

"Holly, why?" Carmen couldn't believe what Holly was asking her.

"Carmen, something doesn't add up."

"Holly, are you kidding me? A two-year-old can add it up!"

"Come on, Carmen." Holly pleaded.

"Holly...we got our butts kicked and almost killed."

"Carmen, we were not the subjects...I mean we weren't the ones having the bad dreams."

"What bad dreams?"

"Joel." Holly was hesitant to speak further.

"Joel...then Joel needs to go out there and face his dreams."

Holly tracked back to the torn-edged photo she put in her purse of the two boys crossing shoulders, expressing a lurking smile.

GABE AND SETH
TAKE A POSE

"Aye boy, don't you see we're takin' a picture...nah git!" The tall dark slim boy looked on anyway as the pictures were being snapped.

That night, Holly began agonizing. She lay in bed with Joel, intensely flipping pages in a magazine back and forth, waiting for the right moment to speak. Holly propped up against the pillow while Joel finished some work on his laptop. As Joel shut down his laptop, Holly looked over towards him. "Did you ever visit your relatives in Beaufort as a child?"

Joel got out of bed and set the laptop on his desk. He walked back, turned the light off and got in bed, "Nope."

"Didn't you ever go visit your great grandfather?"

"Nope."

"Holly, my great grandfather was a number one jackass, and my grandfather and great uncle were even bigger jackasses, alright! Now leave me alone about that."

"He couldn't have been so bad. He left your grandfather 72 acres of land off the coast of Beaufort."

"Yeah, land that nobody in the family wanted."

"What do you mean nobody wanted it?"

"All that beautiful land we left behind along with that damn crazy house – nobody wanted it in my family. My Great Uncle Seth told me that they tried to sell it a couple of times, but after thirty days, the new owners always wanted out, and Uncle Seth didn't bother fighting with them. He would just give them their money back."

"Do you think they experienced what we experienced?"

"They might have and, on the other hand, maybe they found out who Ole man Creech was and didn't want to have anything to do with anything that had his name attached to it."

"Who cares, as long as you are the owner?"

"Ole man Creech was an atheist and a racist, and his sons were rapists. Even his grandson, my father, hated his guts and he didn't know him. My grandmother did the smartest thing by leaving Gabe, that son of a bitch...and that was by taking her only son away from that family. The people in their own town despised them and, that land that was so graciously willed to me – well, nobody wanted it, not even my father, God bless his soul."

"Joel, you talk like you knew him."

"No, that's just all I heard when I was growing up."

"Didn't your great uncle Seth ever find out why the people changed their minds about the land?"

"The only thing I remember hearing was that there was a rumor that the land was sinking."

"What do you mean, sinking?" Holly asks.

"The Atlantic Ocean was moving closer on that part of the land and sometimes the waves would get so big, they would come on shore and bury everything for miles and miles."

"And you wanted to live there?" Carmen asked, shockingly.

"Honey, that was a rumor...Besides, you don't think I would have moved us there if that were true?"

"I hope not."

"Good night."

Fifteen

Back in Beaufort, Holly and Carmen sat idly in the car with the early sea-breeze blowing through their hair. Adoringly, the sun rose up to take its rightful place in the sky. The rushing waves continued to talk to the shore; the conversation was louder than usual, full of conviction, as though it has been aggravated. In the wake of the roaring tidal waves, the house sat, watching.

Holly knew something was seriously wrong with that house. It had everything to do with Joel and she was determined to find out. She tossed her red and blue, faded Atlanta Brave's cap in the back seat of the Jeep Cherokee with a feeling of nostalgia. Carmen got out and stretched her fairly plump arms upward, then leaned forward with her gut inward, followed by sticking her butt outwards with a slight bounce. "I know one thing, whoever built that house here, had a glorious vision in mind."

"What do you mean?" Holly asked.

"I would love to walk out my front door every morning and be greeted by God's most precious gifts. Instead, I greet winos, kicking beer bottles and soda cans out my way."

"That's not a vision. That's a choice you made, Carmen."

"But you know what, Holly? If I really had a choice, I wouldn't be there, now would I?" Holly and Carmen stared at each other in silence.

"Carmen, you made that choice to live there."

"Holly, it's not that...I'm talking about choices that affect our everyday lives and will continue to affect our loved ones or whoever's life we may have touched along the way. Yes, my choice is to live within my means for now, but I know that I'm not going to live there forever. I would love to have a home someday with a white picket fence and a lawn that is so green and flat it's like carpet. I want my children to play in their own backyard, and I want to park my car in a garage." Making her statement very clear to Holly, justifying her attitude, she said, "But that's my choice," tapping her chest with her fingers. "What I'm trying to say is...there are strong reasons why some of us make strong choices. Eventually, our choices will tell a story and it's up to those who are affected by our choices to comprehend the meaning of our stories. Without faith in my choices, I couldn't begin to tell you where it has brought me."

"Carmen, you are the most inspirational person I ever met and I am so delighted Adrian has you in his life. I am so thankful you became my best friend."

"Did you say best friend?"

"Yes."

"You mean, conceited 'Goldie locks' who thinks she's too good to sit at the table with me is not your best friend?"

"I admit, she's got issues, but I don't have to be like her. My choice is to be nice to everyone, whether they are bitches or not."

"Well, Holly. I don't want you just to be nice to me because I already have a lot of nice people in my life." Carmen nodded slightly in return.

"Okay," Holly said in a serious tone. "You wear your clothes way too tight and lipstick is always on your teeth when you smile."

"Holly, I know you didn't go there."

"Don't best friends tell each other the truth?"

"I guess so, but you could have kept that to yourself." Holly and Carmen giggled and embraced each other. Holly saw something as she glanced over Carmen's shoulder.

"Holly, what's wrong?"

Holly saw another house nestled from a distance, in the wooded area with an overgrowth of trees. Their untamed weeds spread high off the ground. If you looked long enough in that direction, you would see the house from a distance. Carmen stared in the direction of Holly's spectacular view. "Okay...Joel's family and Ned weren't the only neighbors around here."

A strange thought had come to Holly. A thought which obviously had some anticipation and that could help get the answers that she so desperately sought. Holly realized that Ned may be the key to Joel's family and the recently discovered house. After all, Ned had to have known something about Joel's family and who lived in the mysterious house. Ned out lived them all; besides he was their neighbor.

"Carmen, I think we need to pay a little visit to Ned."

"How do we know if Ned knew Joel's family and knew who lived in that house?"

"Carmen, look around you...that man is 80-years-old. He has to know something."

It might have taken an hour or so before Holly and Carmen spotted the abandoned house across the way. Boiling fluorescent rays of rainbow colors stretched across the land, revealing the sun's hotness that covered the ocean front. Joel's house and the hidden house were widely separated, overlooking the same ocean.

Holly and Carmen quietly approached the abandoned, fragile square frame that hardly held up the grimy windows. The scenery was army green and brown, and smelled of moist forest pines. A rusted tractor sat out front, an old shredded rope was at rest, tied to one of the branches from the godly, gigantic oak tree that guarded the house. A buttermilk churn occupied the corner of the porch with the stick still inside. Aging spider webs limply hung down and covered the entrance. An old grain beater took its place on the porch, as though it were left intentionally to collect dust.

The only thing that could be heard, at the moment, was the branch leaves wrestling occasionally by the winds. Holly and Carmen could not decide whether or not to step forward towards the daunting house. The more firmly they gripped each other's hands, the more they studied every outside movement that surrounded the house. The decision to move closer was made by the gesture of their bodies, curiously wanting to know what the inside looked like.

Slowly, they continued to take toddler steps towards the front door. Trembling, with sweat seeping out their pores, they prayed and hoped that nothing would greet them. As Holly reached to open what was left of the screen door, black wings the size of an eagle pressed through the slight opening of light leaving feathers drifting in the air. There was a sniveling shriek and crackling of the wood porch floor as Holly and Carmen abruptly fell backwards.

"It's just a bird," Holly said, catching her breath.

"What?" Carmen was flabbergasted at Holly's assertion. "That is not just a bird – that's a sign!"

"A What?" Holly asked, looking fragilely at Carmen.

"A pigeon, a robin, a blue-jay is just a bird." Carmen reiterated.

"Okay, then it's some damn crow."

"Did you not notice the size of that crow?" Carmen's dark brown eyes flared upwards along with her tone of voice.

"Okay, so crows like to eat." Holly said, not sure why Carmen was making a big deal out of the bird.

"Holly, there is no such thing as a crow that damn big. Now let's get the hell out of here!" Carmen demanded.

"Please, Carmen help me." *Silence*. "You're feeling something, aren't you?"

"I'm feeling really scared – right about now, so scared that you are about to be on your own."

"You told me that if I trust in the Lord with all my heart, acknowledge Him, He will direct my path. Carmen I trust Him. We can stand up and face anything or anyone."

"Yes Holly, that's right. I'm facing you in this mosquito and fly infested trap that's been hidden behind these wild, growing, leaning trees for centuries, not to mention inhaling dust mites that are carrying all kind of diseases!" Changing the tone of her voice from soft to hard.

"Carmen please...I can't do this without you. Joel is all I have."

The heat alone was enough to suffocate an elderly person, and the putrid odor stuck all over Holly and Carmen like someone painted their body with feces. The smell of decomposed rodents turned their stomachs, while clumps of dead flies rested on every flat service in the house. This made it impossible to breathe without throwing up.

For a moment, Carmen was apprehensive about going near the house. Holly watched and listened out for every movement by the house. Curiously, Holly paced towards the brick stove, or what was left of it, and realized that a woman's presence occupied this home, once upon a time.

Holly absorbed Carmen's body language. "Carmen, what are you feeling?"

"Can you not see me? Did you not hear me, and you still ask me a question like that?"

"Come on...whatever spirit that is lurking these grounds connected with you that night in the kitchen."

"All I know is that we are not wanted here and we have to go now!"

"Are we not wanted in this house or Joel's house?"

"Good question...I don't know." Carmen said softly.

Carmen slowly nestled her face in the palms of her hands and took two deep breaths. She intently looked around the house and saw objects that reminded her of her own past.

"My great grandmother used to have an iron like that. If I had to use this iron now, I would never make it to work on time."

"Yeah, and if I had to iron with that iron, nothing would get pressed."

The mangled weeds pierced through the open cracks of the splintered floor, and the windows were covered in streaks of dirt. This gave every indication that no one had lived here for a very long time.

Carmen recognized a grimy, what-used-to-be white apron, hanging beside the broken stone fireplace. She folded her hands together, as though she were about to pray, then she walked over and touched it. Carmen studied the apron and felt an eerie sensation. Suddenly, her legs buckled and she collapsed to the floor. Holly rushed to her side, helping her back on her feet. "What's wrong?"

"Holly, we have to leave," said Carmen weakly. Carmen's face showed fear. She wept helplessly, shielding her speech.

"Carmen, whoever is around here, WE ARE NOT AFRAID OF YOU!" Holly shouted up towards the ceiling.

Blood began to drip out of Carmen's nose. "Carmen, I'm so sorry, let's get out of here." Swiftly, Holly looked around the house and helped Carmen to her feet, pacing towards the door.

All of a sudden, Carmen stopped in her tracks. She noticed a frame on the wall with distinct carvings. She didn't see a picture right away, but desperately wanted to take a closer look at the picture frame on the wall. They had drawn away from the front door, up closer to the heavy oval frame. Holly carefully reached for the picture and took it off the fragile wall, blowing the dust off and handing it to Carmen. Carmen was still holding her shirt up to her nose. She freed one arm to wipe away the many centuries that covered the heavy glass frame. She wiped away the last cover of dust and looked as though she'd seen a ghost. Holly stood firmly by Carmen and her jaw dropped as she stared past the reflection of the glass.

"It's a family portrait."

"And look who's in it," Holly said

"Well, I'll be..." Carmen said through her shirt.

Late that afternoon, they camped on the porch of the house that once had been home to Joel and Holly. Holly thought they would be safe if they stayed outside most of the time.

"Carmen, I am so sorry for getting you in this."

"All I know is that if I don't make it back home alive and in time for my wedding – you will be sorry." Giggles and friendly gestures took over the thought of being scared earlier.

The sky held enough light for Holly and Carmen to decide what they were going to do next, considering they still had no answers, only a picture.

Looking out beyond sea level, Carmen's silent thought absorbed a frightening intuition – it told her this land kept company of someone who lived here long ago. No one knew who or why that someone had not passed over.

"Holly, this place holds something fierce with anger, and it can't leave from here," Carmen said calmly, gazing towards the ocean.

Exhausted, Holly slapped her face and it soon rushed with blood. Sobbing. "Okay, Carmen. Why Joel? Joel has never been here before. He's never lived here before, up until last month. He never knew his father's side of the family – for crying out load, he recently found out about his great uncle Seth, and that's because Joel is the only living relative left."

Out of desperation, Holly stood up and walked to the front door. Angrily, she opened the door and dashed inside the house. "WHAT DO YOU WANT?" She screamed at the top of her voice. "COME AND GET ME!" Holly became motionless. "WELL COME ON – HERE'S YOUR CHANCE!"

Carmen quietly stood in the doorway, feeling sorry for Holly. "Holly, it's not you it wants...you have no roots here." Slowly, Carmen tiptoed toward Holly, grabbed her hand. "Let's go, Holly...we have to go." As soon as Holly and Carmen stepped outside onto the front porch – the door slammed shut, narrowly hitting them on the butt.

"Gee, Holly, you didn't have to slam the door."

"Carmen, I didn't touch the door."

Holly and Carmen's eyes were wide open, shining with fright. Their faces scowled in dismay.

"It knows we're here," Carmen said dismally. "The wind is not strong enough," Carmen said, feeling the air. Carmen touched the heavy oak door with the palm of her hand then eased her hand down onto the door knob to open it. The door was locked. Carmen and Holly's eyes were inseparable. Stillness hung between them for two minutes, more curious than frightened. At last, Carmen's eyes blinking saw fire burning on Ned's land.

"Holly, how could all this be going on and your neighbor wasn't affected by it?"

"How do we know he wasn't?"

"Look around you." Carmen held her arms out by her side. "There's only three houses on this side of the island. Mr. Ned is the only one who lives in any of the houses."

"Come to think of it, isn't Mr. Ned on Joel's property?" Holly asked.

"It's time we pay Mr. Ned a little visit."

The moonlight recovered on the island's east shoreline whereas the fading ocean soon became stationary. Not even a gust of wind could be felt.

Barrels of fire were crackling, dispersing ashes in space. Ned sat peacefully, his hazy dark eyes fixed on the ocean.

"Remember Ah got eyes in de back of mah head," Ned said never shifting his head.

Stunned, Holly and Carmen stared at each other.

"Ah'see yuh come back," Ned said, showing his coffee stained teeth with tartar build up.

"Yes, Mr. Ned. I wanted to know if I can ask you a few questions about our house."

"So you brought yo' friend back too," Ned said, tilting his cap forward, never meeting Holly and Carmen's eyes.

"Oh, where's my manners...this is my best friend, Carmen," Holly emphasized with pleasure.

"Yes, we've met."

"You know that night when Joel wasn't feeling so well," Carmen said, watching Holly for acknowledgment.

"Oh yes, how I could forget about the nightmare from hell. Interestingly, that's what we want to talk to you about."

Slowly, Ned lifted his head just enough to glance at Holly. "Was it a dream or a nightmare?"

"Dream? Nightmare? It's all the same," Holly said.

"For God speaketh once, yea twice, yet man perceiveth it not." Carmen started to recite with Ned, "In a dream, in a vision of night, when deep sleep falleth upon men, in slumberings upon the bed, then He openeth the ears of men and sealeth their instructions....Job, 33:14."

Holly tried to keep her face expressionless. She didn't want Carmen and Ned to know that she wasn't familiar with the scriptures in the Bible. "So basically, God is trying to tell Joel something through his dreams."

Ned finally looked up from the ground and asked Holly, "Is dat why Joel left?"

"No, Mr. Ned. We left that house because the house is haunted and something or someone was trying to drive my fiancé crazy!"

Ned spoke tenderly, "It's not Gawd."

"Well then, who?" Holly waved her hands in the air.

"Where's Joel, nah?" Ned asked, gazing back down at the ground.

"He's home in Georgia." Holly replied.

"No, he's not." Ned said.

"Mr. Ned, you seem to know more about my fiancé than I do," Holly said, coldly.

Ned steadily raised his right arm in front of him and pointed northward to the back splash of the ocean's scenery.

"Oh my goodness! Joel and Adrian, what are you doing here?"

"We thought you two could use some more hands." Joel and Holly embraced each other. Holly and Carmen were so excited to see Joel and Adrian that they didn't notice Ned's quiet disappearance into the darkness.

Sixteen

Joel grinded his teeth while sucking his face in as he squeezed his narrow buttocks, striding to the front door. Sweat trickled down the back of his neck like dripping icicles. In fact, he wished, in a brief reverie, that he could be at another place and time, but knew if an answer was going to be revealed, it had to be now.

Holly glaringly stared at Joel as he continued to move forward. She was hesitant for Joel to turn the door knob. "You guys, instead, let's go out to dinner tonight and stay in a hotel. We can pack in the morning and get the hell out of here."

Joel narrowed his eyes and dropped his head, then slowly turned to look at Holly. A silent message of "I love you" was sent without an utter. Joel turned the door knob. The blood in Joel's veins throbbed like an overworked pump as he moved through the house. His thumping heart drowned his hearing. Holly called out to him, "Joel...Joel...Joel." He never looked back.

Taking a deep breath, Joel stepped in the house. He strolled through the house, carefully taking notice of the old picture frames on the walls, and an elderly ebony-framed mantle mirror sitting on the floor, leaning against the wall in a corner of the living room. As soon as he saw the light blinking on and off in the kitchen, he knew that whatever it was, it was waiting for him. As he reached the kitchen doorway, he took a deep breath and swallowed hard. Joel looked up at the dim-lighted chandelier that was hoisted up in the ceiling and steadied it as it rocked back and forth. Strange bright lights disbursed in the kitchen then blinked off, then on, then off. It was as though the blinking lights were blinking on and off as part of a game.

The lights stayed off. Joel opened his eyes wide, trying to see in the dark, feeling his way through the empty kitchen while gasping for breath. He panicked and quickly tried to find a light switch on the wall, but stumbled. His body slammed down to the floor, like a hardcover book thrown against a hard surface. He was unconscious for a moment.

At once, the house came alive. Lightning held the house hostage and the wild winds came uninvited over the land. The thick branches on the leaning trees touched the floor of the island without leaving a shadow underneath. There was sharp thunder over the house, hard enough to wake Joel. Coming to, he noticed the kitchen chandelier lights flickering sporadically and voices of laughter echoing in the background.

Ned, standing before the throttling ocean rushing over his feet, confronted the restless waves and pleaded as sincerely as he could. "Please leav'em alone. Take me, it's mah fault...dey ain't done nothin'." Just then, the sky ripped open its heart, swallowing the bright fantasies, and then puking out thundering sparks of nightmares. It gushed out like the world's biggest lightning storm. The unleashed uproarious rumble blustered underneath the waves, sifting the sand beneath Ned's feet, shaking him lightly.

Back at the lively house, turning over from his fall, his face darkened with blood, Joel struggled to his feet. "Dear God, please help me," he cried at the lighted chandelier. An unusual discrete accent tapped in Joel's hearing as he wobbled on his tired legs. This voice was the only thing to be heard, a voice without familiarity. Unable to maintain his independence and his ability to take charge of his five senses, Joel thought to himself, "I can't see." His frustration was smeared, although he could sense something evil was about to share his space.

"Why have you come here?"

Quickly, Joel took his eyes away from the drowning lights to follow the cracked voice diagonally across the kitchen. "Sweet Mother of Jesus!" Joel said with fright, registering the monstrous sight before him, eyes bulging and jaws hanging. "Who are you?" A large unworldly figure stood inches away.

"Who are you?" Joel asked again, shakily.

The house started rumbling and heavy pulsation shocks came underneath the floors into Joel's body. Stacked boxes flew on the floor, breaking dishes while furniture flew across the room, shattering against the walls.

The house that breathed death came alive. Joel was trembling with anger because the nameless thing started to move inches closer towards him. "Please tell me, what do you want?" He was crying and shouting desperately, spit flinging out the sides of his mouth.

Without warning, the snarling, black hefty-figured, wicked thing rushed up to Joel's face, breathing in his frightened breath. A deathly-figured body, with strings of seaweed hanging out of its oversized raw pores and frail bones were clearly visible at the skin's surface. Joel was too scared to look directly into the black-eyed gruesome face that stood before him. The horrifying darkness that covered him was about to remind him of why he was there.

"Get off this land," hissed the unknown spirit. Before Joel could respond, muddy floods of foul-smelling black water gushed forcefully out of every water pipe and spout in and outside of the house, detaching the fixtures from their places. The voluble deep-sea mixed with its bowels and marina greenery soil filled the house like a reservoir.

Joel stood paralyzed in knee-deep water that continued to rise. He could feel the presence of the sea-wood fiend's face near his frightened body. Thunder rattled the earth even more, shaking the house. By this time, the water level was steadily rising. He stumbled as he tried to get to freedom and accidentally swallowed the water.

There was another ripping sound that bellowed over the thunder. A scream, a horrifying struggle. Joel thought of Holly. He struggled toward the front door, opened it. He was met by an enormous black wave, rushing straight towards him. The wave struck Joel's body like an uprooted tree, flushing him down in a deep bloody forest.

AUGUST 29, 1943

The sun had matured above the white, and nearly blue, canvas, picturing a perfect horizon. At the same time, the heat matted the sawdust on the floor inside the wooded, general store. Joseph finally made it to the store. He picked up a sack of flour as his mother requested then descended towards the counter. He slammed it down in front of ole man Creech.

'Courage.' A word that taunted Joseph growing up. He knew he still didn't have it. All the things he wanted to do or say that would make him feel better became imprisoned in his mind, not sure they would ever be freed. As a result, he turned out to be his own prisoner, so afraid to be liberated.

Joseph's head curled downward even more. Disgusted at his lack of guts, he smashed his fist down on the counter then opened his fingers, letting go of copper pennies and steel nickels. Ole man Creech's stare was locked on Joseph. He didn't even count the change; he just ogled Joseph, not saying a word. Joseph barely lifted up his head to sneak a quick look at ole man Creech's face; that was all it took for Joseph to cut into his nippy gaze.

Heedless to his surroundings, Joseph darted out the front door of the general store with Rosa Lee's sack of flour for Lula's birthday cake. He started out on the nature trail that led near the pathway on the shoulder of his home where he once lived. He heard drowning voices between the jam-packed greenery and lofty trees. He slowed down but kept walking. Without warning, he snapped his head in position, keeping his wary eyes in the direction of the heavy whispering voices. Seth and Gabe were hovering in secrecy.

Like a ghost, Joseph stopped in his tracks to eavesdrop closely. Steadily trying to hold his body still, Joseph lost his balance and stepped on a patch of dried branches. The

crackling sound was loud enough for Seth and Gabe to look up. Instead of denying what Joseph may have overheard, they included him, as though Joseph was there all the time.
    "Hey, Joseph."
    "Hey!"
    "We got somethin' yuh wunt."
    "Wut?"
    "How'd yuh lak tuh get yo' pa's land back?"
    Joseph eyes widened like a crystal ball. "Wut you know 'bout mah daddy's land?"
    "We know yo' momma lost it and would do anything tuh get it back."
    "Don't talk 'bout mah momma!"
    "Now com'on, we ain't talkin' 'bout your momma, we jis' know ole Rose Lee haven't been de same since yo' dadduh died and had to get off dat land. Joseph dis is yo' lucky day."
    "What ya'll talkin' bout?"
    "You see's dis." Seth waved the deed to James's land in Joseph's face. "Ah got wut you and yo' momma wunt."
    "We know yo' dadduh stole mah dadduh's land." Joseph pouted.

"Naw Joseph, mah dadduh don't steal. Neither do we, but Gabe and I are prepared tuh make an offuh yuh can't refuse."

"What kind of offuh?"

"You got uh hundred dollars?"

Meanwhile, Lula was at the general store. Gallantly, she approached the store counter with a smile almost touching her eyes.

"And jis' what yuh're so damn happy about," asked ole man Creech in a harsh tone.

"Teday's mah birthday." She twitched her waist from side to side, showing off her hand-made dress sewed with hand-me-down material, but decent fabric.

"Well, what yuh wunt?"

"A sucker." Ole man Creech reached for the box of suckers and handed one to Lula. Lula slammed her penny down at the same time that she grabbed her sucker out of ole man Creech's hand. She dashed out the store. Lula followed the same path as Joseph. As she was slowly walking and twisting the wrapper off her sucker, she heard Joseph's voice. "He

still ain't got home... Oooh Momma's gonna to tear his tail up," she said to herself.

Lula quietly moved in closer to Joseph's voice and picked up other voices. She was shocked to find, it was Seth and Gabe. She was more curious to find out what Joseph was doing with Seth and Gabe, more than anything else. Her last step brushed the dirt pebbles harder than expected. Quickly she said, "Didn't Momma tell yuh tuh git back wid her flour?"

"Mine yo' business and git home, Lula!" Joseph snapped, raising his voice to be heard through the trees.

"Ah'm tellin' Momma."

Seth noticed her like a commodity, for which all young boys would temporarily yearn. Lula rolled her eyes at the vile stare and turned away to skip back home.

Joseph knew he couldn't come up with that kind of money. Seth and Gabe knew it too. Joseph went ahead and agreed to it anyway. Joseph grabbed a chance to make his mother proud of him. Rosa Lee and Lula would finally look up to him.

"You know he ain't got no hundred dollars." Gabe said as he and Seth walked back through the trail to the general store.

"Yeah...but he's so damn stupid he'll find a way."

"Pa will kill you if he finds out dat you 'bout sold James's land back to his son."

"Who says we're sellin' it back to his son?"

"You jis' told Joseph..."

"Who cares what I told 'Jo Boy', how you think Pa got everything we got."

Although Lula's mother, Rosa Lee, ordered her to stay off ole man Creech's land, Lula pranced all the way to the dock that connected to the earth. She was determined to continue to inhale the ocean's natural splendor. Especially now, considering what she overheard Seth and Gabe talking to Joseph about. The truth had been leaked. Shock wasn't inevitable, it was downright pitiful.

Lula crouched at the edge of the dock as though it were her lawful seat. She expressed her deepest thoughts, melting her sucker around her tongue. Almost matured thoughts drifted along the summer air, blended with the overwhelming smell of seaweed resting beneath the beams of the dock. Still sucking, she gazed at her watery image distorted in the supple current. Lula cleared her throat, gulping down her last quench of sugar. She tossed the naked stick on top of the waters' cover, gaping at it as it floated steadily on top of her reflection mirrored by the water.

"Ah knows yo're dare," she said grinning. Suddenly, Lula heard footsteps and got up and looked around. By this time, Seth and Gabe were already on the dock, walking towards her. Lula stood straight up.

"Didn't yo' Momma ever teach yuh not tuh go on other people's property widout dare permission?"

"Dis ain't yo' property," Lula lashed back at Seth.

"Dis here our land," Gabe said.

"You ain't got no land. Yo' Pa stole it from mah Dadduh," Lula boldly spoke.

"Why you little ease droppin' rusty bitch...Git!" By this time, Seth's bitterness was spilling all over him.

Lula slowly walked between Seth and Gabe. Seth was boiling at that point and wanted the last word. "No damn gal is 'gon talk lak dat to me!"

Seth started off behind her and Gabe grabbed him. "Let it go, ain't nobody suppose tuh know."

"She knows, besides our asses are jis' as good as dead anywaze, let's enjoy ourselves while we can."

"Whutcha talkin' 'bout?" Gabe said, confused.

"Watch!" Seth quickly paced himself ahead of Lula and jumped in front of her, blocking her way. Abruptly, he shoved her on the shoulder so hard it knocked her down. "Ah'm gonna show yuh somethin' Ah do got." Seth pulled his dingy overall straps off his shoulders then down by his waist.

"Seth no!" Gabe said, pleading.

Lula tried to get up and Seth knocked her back down on the dock. "Yo' brother said he would pay us fuh dis land and since we ain't got paid

yet, Ah'll take mah pay right nah."
Seth pinned his body on top of Lula,
pressing his weight down on top of
her, slapping her furiously in the face
until blood pierced her cheeks. Lula,
terrified, weeped.

Gabe hysterically looked around
to make sure no one was in sight,
blocking his ears from the scream of
horror. "She ain't got no money, she
ain't got no money!"

"She doesn't need any."

"Seth, don't do dis...let's git outta
here."

"Shut up and stop bein' a damn
wimp and get some pussy!" *As the*
brothers argued, Lula struggled to get
up enough strength to get out from
underneath Seth. Gabe grabbed her,
fleshing his body all over hers. Seth
said, "dare yuh'go bro...dis yo'
day...git it while yuh can!"

It wasn't too long before Gabe
gave in. He wanted Lula to stop
screaming, so he covered her mouth
and joined his brother's impious ways.

"Nah, we gettin' paid."

Seth and Gabe took turns
maliciously tasting and robbing Lula's

petite flesh that had been hidden for thirteen years. Lula's screams diffused throughout the humid air.

Beaten and raped on the dock, with only the Atlantic as a witness, she could hardly breathe or see. As soon as Seth and Gabe's violent deed was fulfilled, they took off running. Lula scuffled to get to her feet, effortlessly balancing herself. She looked up towards the land and noticed a dark image standing in the far distance. She focused her swollen eyes and did all she could to take one step closer. She saw her brother's image, barely visible, through the swelling around her eyes. Joseph stood barely at the head of the dock, reserved and not moving. Lula put her head down, slowly turned around to look in the water's eyes for serenity. She dragged herself to the edge of the dock and stepped off.

In the kitchen where he had begun, underneath the ancient chandelier swaying back and forth, Joel knew he had to get to Holly very quickly. He opened his eyes in a freaked-out zone, then grabbed his head and realized he was drenched. As he cringed on the floor, surrounded in huge puddles of black volatile water, he started to vomit. It had been like going down into the deep, beyond the surface, not knowing the way out and fighting for air. He tried to hold onto a good rationalization and in a minute or two - it eventually came to him. It was fact that gave him the ability to know the difference between a dream and reality. Joel was no longer able to withstand the horror that agonized his soul over something unknown to him, and he wanted it gone.

Joel drunkenly stood to his feet and staggered out of the kitchen. He slipped in the black puddles that spilled over from his real-life nightmare, got up, and rushed down the hall to the front door as fast as he could, puking fright all over himself. He turned the doorknob in panic, only to be greeted by a brilliant white moon.

"Holly, Holly, Holly, Adrian, Adrian, Carmen!" Frantically, he hollered out their names while circling around the house.

A settled voice tuned into Joel's hollering. "Dey ain't heah."

"Where are they?" Joel shouted, out of breath.

"Ah'll take yuh tuh dem."

"You will take me nowhere. Now tell me where is Holly and my friends!"

"Ah know all dis may be uh bit strange tuh yuh but please calm down, Ah can explain."

Breathless with exhaustion, Joel fell to his knees out of desperation and started to cry, "You're that boy aren't you?"

"Dat all depends on whut boy yuh're talkin' 'bout."

"Why are you doing this?"

"Joel Ah'm not doin' anything. Ah've lived wid dis since I wuz a chile and if I could do anything 'bout it, Ah'd done so uh long time ago."

"Why is she hunting me?" Joel cries out, chopping has hands into his chest.

"First, lemme take yuh tuh Holly and yo' friends, then Ah'll explain."

An old ceiling fan made a feeble attempt to circulate the stifling enclosed air. Silence poured over a pot of hot tea and anxiety dripped down from the mouths of nonbelievers, who now believed. Joel's fifteen minutes with the horrid thing seemed like centuries running away from death, death propelled by Joel's ancestors in times of yore.

Seventeen

After revealing Joel's ancestral connection with his family, Ned stood up from his worn-out duck-taped recliner chair. He sincerely looked deep into Joel's glossy blue eyes, "Ah'm dat boy. Mah name is Joseph Ned Kannon and James wuz mah fadduh. Rosa Lee wuz mah mudduh and Lula wuz mah sistuh." Joseph walked toward the aged wooden panel screen door, quietly glancing out, consumed with emotions of emptiness and shame. Carmen stared blankly as she followed Joseph to the door, "Mr. Joseph, what does she want from you?"

"Ah'd thought it wuz mah soul, but Ah tried many times...still Ah'm heah."

"Then it's not your spirit she wants."

"Ah've suffered fo' 64 years and sufferin' nah."

"Then it's not satisfaction she wants."

"Y'all, Ah killed mah'own sistuh," he wept frantically. "Ah wuz so damn skade tuh he'p mah'own sistuh. Ah'd coulda done somethin', but no...Ah froze...Ah froze...Deah Gawd please fo'give me." Joseph gasped his breath along with his 'I should of', and then dropped his head down in his hands.

Carmen, at that moment, didn't know whether to console him or give him space. As soon as she put her hand up to touch his left shoulder, Joseph pushed open the screen door and gaped at the picturesque waves. Carmen quickly turned to look at Joel, Adrian and Holly, and then swiftly followed Joseph with her eyes. "Joseph, I know I wasn't there, but Lula's rape and death is not your fault."

"Yes, it is," he managed to say before his lungs exploded. "Ah should had gone straight tuh Momma soon as Ah found out ole man Creech stole dadduh's land. But no, Ah wanted tuh make Momma proud of me when Ah got dadduh's land back. Ah should have known Seth and Gabe nevuh was goin' tuh give me de original deed back, even if Ah had uh hundred dollars. Momma alwaze knew somethin' wuz terribly wrong wid ole man Creech's story; he said mah dadduh didn't pay'em back. Momma knew, deep down, dadduh alwaze paid his debts. We didn't have de means tuh fight back fo' whut wuz rightfully ours – dey knew it and dat's how'd come dey jis' took it."

Joel, Holly and Adrian were standing with Joseph and Carmen on the porch. "Yuh'see, out dere," pointing towards the house his father built and the open air towards the waves. "Mah fo' parents walked out dere, dey jis' walked like nothin' could stop dem."

"They walked where?" asked Holly, a little confused. Joseph pointed his wrinkled-aged, ashy index finger straight forward. "You mean out there?" Holly was still trying to make sense of what Joseph was saying.

"Mah dadduh used tuh tell us stories of his people. Dey were Kings and Queens in Africa and slaves heah. Mah great great-grandfather gathered up his people here on dis very land, not even fifty steps away from where we're standin'. He walked tuh freedom. Mah great grandfather wuz scared and stayed behind. He wuz left tuh tell de stories of our people. He eventually walked out dere too."

"You mean, he just walked out to the Atlantic Ocean and drowned?" Holly asked with disbelief.

"No, dey walked tuh freedom. Silence surrounded them. Dem not dead; dey live lak you and me, except dem out dere," Joseph said, looking forward, bobbing his head up and down.

"Jeez." Joel stared at him glassily. "So they've been watching us the whole time?"

Joseph started again. "Ah remember when Ah wuz uh little boy, my grand dadduh come tuh us late in de hour. He told mah dadduh he wuz sorry fuh bringin' him into uh world where a man has tuh fight or die fuh de breath God gave him. You see...Grand dadduh stayed long enough tuh meet his next generation and, off he went too. He could no longer stomach de evil way-of-life congregated by man, not by God. Left behind were de ones who became witness tuh our fo' folks' existence. For us, freedom wuz uh passage of sovereignty, uh means of accessing free will widout restrictions dat should have never been placed upon any man or woman nor a child in de first place. We are all one. I jis' think it's a shame dat some of us don't understand dat. Mah people's freedom lies in the belly of de earth. Yuh see, earth is our cradle from de beginning. We are special underneath de sun; mah fadduh said it wuz God's highest angel, a ball of fire in uh circle, so dat de angel can see whut we are doin'. Then it goes away, forming into half circles and whole circles of white light, disguising itself while we sleep. You ever heard de saying, 'God is watchin' yuh no matta where you are and whatcha doin', he can see yuh at all times." Chuckling. "Yes indeed, yuh betta b'lieve dat."

"Joseph, I understand that ole man Creech wrongly took James' receipt off his dead body and his sons brutally raped Lula, but what does that have to do with Joel?" Carmen asks.

"His blood runs wid ole man Creech, Seth and Gabe's. Lula lives off dere dried up blood which dusts wickedness all through her bones. She lives fo' revenge."

Adrian felt his pulse start to race. "I'll have you to know that Joel doesn't have an ounce of bad blood in his body. He's the utmost decent human being I know."

"It duzn't matta. His family line stems from ole man Creech. Lula's spirit roams in de darkness; she's in uh deep sleep. She's restless wid vengeance and seeks out de evil dat harbored on dis land in 1943. No one could stay on dis land, wid'out sleepin wid Lula."

"But still, what does all of this have to do with Joel?" Carmen asks again.

"Joel is de last survivin' blood of de Creechs'. It duzn't matta if he wuz around den or not, nor if he's a good person. His blood runs through dis land lak de red swirled 'round on a mint candy."

Carmen walked over to the other side of the porch with a lonely feeling and sat in the old rocking chair. She fixed her eyes on the open space neighboring the ocean and began to weep. Holly, Joel, and Adrian followed her emotional tears, approaching her concerns. She held her hand out to where a beam of warmth from the sun interfered within the open air. Locking her autumn brown eyes to Joel's, she was barely able to breathe. "Joel, you have to end this with Lula."

"How?"

"You have to make it right; you're the only one who can stop her vengeance."

"How?" Joel asks, this time with a fluctuating voice.

"I don't know," said Carmen, staring into Joseph's eyes.

"I don't know either," sighed Holly, trying to hold back tears. The unknown answer went from face to face.

Eighteen

Joel's trembling hands unruffled his denim shirt collar and then raked his golden clumpy hair. He stood, solitary, in front of the house that once belonged to Joseph's family. He transitioned his eyes forward and said, "Lula this is between you and me...well let's finish it."

"You're not going back in there, are you?" Holly surprisingly walked behind Joel.

"No, I think am going to get to know my neighborhood first."

"How are you going to do that?"

"Beaufort's Historical Archives."

Joel and Holly drove into town, discovering more sites than they had before, during their short-lived stay in Beaufort. The Atlantic had begun to disappear as they drove west. The closer they got inland, the louder the streets became. The smell of all types of fish took over the ocean's air. There were open markets spread throughout town.

Joel and Holly's stomachs were growling at one another, so they decided to get lunch. They stopped at a restaurant that resembled a log cabin. It had a country feel with granny rocking chairs lined in front as you walked in the doors. The inside was spacious and a big fireplace was nestled in the rear by the kitchen's swinging doors. Since it was summer time, it was already cozy and warm inside. The southern waitress greeted every customer with an old-fashioned hospitality that would invite them to come back again. The walls were covered with old pictures in old frames – you felt like you were eating back in time.

"Good afternoon and welcome to Millie's House in the South. Can I start you with a cup of coffee?"

"Two decafs please."

"Joel, can you imagine what it must have been like living around here, way back in the day?"

"Please...what do you think I've been doing with Lula?"

"Oh yeah, I'm sorry."

"I never wanted to be associated with my father's family, and now I am," Joel said, clearly upset.

"Joel, we can't make choices about who we come from, we just have to make sure we don't become them."

"Holly, almost 65 years ago, in this town my great grandfather stole 72-acres of land from a good man. On top of that, he deprived this man's family of an inheritance that's rightfully theirs. So now, ole man Creech's evil still walks on this land, still breathes in the air and still lives after all these years. His sons; Gabe, my grandfather, and Seth my great uncle, brutally raped his daughter. Hell...you might as well say they killed her. For Christ's Sake we degraded this man's family and his daughter is pissed off!" he said in a murmuring tone.

"Joel, you didn't do any of that."

"Tell that to Lula. She's not going to let up until I'm dead."

"Joel, let's think for a minute here. When Lula speaks to you, she wants you off the land, right? So why not give Joseph back the deed, that way you will not be tied to the land anymore."

"Why does that sound so easy and how come no one after all these years thought of that? And how do you suppose we fix Lula's death?" Joel replied sarcastically and with an indication of being overwhelmed.

"There's got to be a way to rectify Joseph's family's 72 acres and Lula's forgiveness."

Suddenly, Joel's eyes bulged out of his sockets, jaw wide open. "Holly, look! It's Lula!" His swelling eyes stared straight ahead at an old black and white photo in an oval bronze frame hanging above the fireplace.

Joel and Holly jumped up from their chairs and walked over to the fireplace to get a closer look. Joel quickly grabbed his pocket and pulled out a black and white snapshot of Lula. He reached up and placed the 4x7 picture in his hand beside the framed photograph on the wall. The resemblance was astonishing.

The rosy-cheeked chubby waitress walked by, "There you are, your coffee is on the table. Are you ready to order?"

Joel couldn't take his eyes off the photographs to answer. Holly asked, "How can we find out who this young girl is?"

"We can't...these are old orphan pictures from the old timers that were passed down from the locals years and years ago. Miss Mildred who we call Millie, the owner, started this restaurant. She asked neighbors and friends for their ancestors' pictures to put up on the walls...She wanted an old time environment with old fashion cookin'."

"Do you think Millie would know who this girl was?"

"Don't know...Miss Millie is in a nursing home now and she doesn't talk much anymore. Although, she does have a niece that checks in on her regularly. She's a student at Savannah University and works part-time at the Hampton library during the summer."

"Can you please tell us where we can find her niece?"

"Sure...Only if you promise to come back and chow down on some of this good ole cookin'."

"You bet!"

Joel opened the heavy glass doors for Holly and they both stepped into the hollow, spacious, front area of the library. As they walked in, they seemed dwarfed by the 100 carrels with high walls. A big sign hung below the information desk with red bold letters that made it overly-recognized: PLEASE REFRAIN FROM CONVERSATION. Joel and Holly anxiously walked up to the front desk and whispered, "May we please speak with Laurie Porter?"

"Just one moment please," the hunchbacked, wrinkled-face man replied. As he picked up the telephone, his green spider-webbed veins protruded visibly through his skin. He had a nerve condition or he was on medication, because his hands were steadily shaking. "You can wait in the meeting room down the hall on the right."

Joel and Holly couldn't pass up the opportunity to sit in the plush mahogany, cloth chairs that bordered the cherry wood conference room table. In spite of recognizing the luxurious meeting room accommodations, Joel was still anxious to make a connection to Lula. He gawked at an old picture of Beaufort's water frontier, painted in the early nineteenth century. The second he got up to take a closer look at the author's name, a voice rushed in, "Hello, may I help you?"

"I know you from somewhere, don't I?"

"Oh my gosh, yes! We met in the grocery store parking lot."

"Yes, how are you?"

Holly looked at Joel with an unbreakable stare, waiting to be introduced. "Oh yes, this is my fiancée, Holly."

"Hello, it's nice to meet you."

"Likewise."

"I thought your name was Erin?" Joel recanted.

"Well yes – that's my middle name. Since I was the last of four girls and my dad and mom was shooting to have a boy – I became Erin Laurie Porter. I use 'Erin' with a masculine charm, if you know what I mean."

"We get it," Holly said, laughing.

"So how can I help you?"

"We saw a picture of this young girl hanging up in your great aunt's diner."

"Aunt Millie rarely talks, especially not to strangers. She's stubborn in that way. Can I see this picture?" Joel reached in his back pocket and pulled out the picture. Erin stared at it, thinking that the likelihood of her aunt recognizing this person was a slim chance to none. "I really can't help you with this one, and I'm not sure if my Aunt Millie will be able to either. But I'll be glad to take you to her during my lunch break."

"Thank you."

"Do you mind if I ask why you want to know this girl's name?"

"Well...we actually know her name. We wanted to know who she was."

"May I ask why?"

"Lula, James and my grandfather and great uncle were neighbors and I'm doing some ancestry research. We found out that they lived in her family's home, which I inherited."

"Why is the research on Lula and not your relatives?"

Joel stood speechless and stared at Holly, waiting for her to interrupt his silence. "We're looking for anyone who can share whatever they know about the house."

"You might want to have all your questions ready or written down for Aunt Millie. Don't expect to get all your answers, if any, in one day. I break in ten minutes. Meet me back at the information desk."

Nineteen

At the nursing home, Joel felt the sensation of butterflies fluttering in his gut. Not only were his nerves nestled in his stomach, but he held in his urine during the whole trip there. Stepping towards the double wooden doors, he bent over, gripping the rail. "Are you alright?" Erin asked, stopping in her tracks.

"Don't mind me. I need to make a pit stop to the boy's room."

"Sure thing. The rest rooms are on the right as soon as we enter the doors. I'll sign us in and we'll meet you in room 104."

Joel zealously speed-walked down the white lengthy hall where the polished floors looked like slippery ice, maneuvering past wheelchairs and empty bed carts parked along the walls. Steadily moving, he curiously stared into the eyes of the elderly, thinking to himself, one day my time will come...where will I be and who will care for me? The more that feeling sunk in, the more rapidly Joel paced down the sallow hall, contemplating his aging destiny.

As he continued to walk forward, he came upon an old lady in a wheelchair. It was parked in the middle of Joel's path that led to his destination. She had one sock on that barely reached above her ankle, and the other foot was resting on the wheelchair's foot pedestal. He couldn't help but notice that she stared at him with vastness, as though he were some kind of political figure. The corners of her mouth were sucked in and had just about disappeared. Her eyes were hoary grey, although her gaze at Joel was clearly visible. She never took her tired eyes off him, even when he turned his attention away for a quick second. Being the kind of man Joel was – he slowed down and met her stare.

Complete silence spilled over their stare like super glue on paper. Joel stood in front of this frail living being as though he had been hypnotized. Joel was gazing steadily at a native of Beaufort, South Carolina. He shamefully noticed his lengthy stare and faintly spoke, "Hello," with a wave then swiftly walked away.

149

Right away, Erin tidied the room up, dumped the bed pan, then rolled the white sheets up and back down on the bed. She took the vase of thirsty flowers sitting on the table next to the bed into the bathroom and ran water in it. Joel was in the room by this time. He stood next to Holly, quietly staring at this frail soul with white long hair that shone like silk. Age-spotted hands crossed over each other in her lap. All that could be seen were the decades of wrinkles pressed on her delicate skin.

"Aunt Millie, you have company today," Erin shouted aloud. Joel and Holly stepped closer to Millie.

"Whatcha say?" Millie asked, in a scratching low voice.

Erin spoke louder. "Meet Joel and Holly, they want to talk to you, but first, they want to show you a picture." Holly's eyes widened and looked at Joel for him to pull out the photograph.

"Hello, my name is Joel Lee Keys, this is my fiancée, Holly."

"How you?" Slowly, she raised her head to glance at Joel then, bit by bit, turned her head towards Holly.

Joel kneeled before Millie, holding up the 4x7 picture closely for her to acknowledge.

"Aunt Millie, do you know who this person is in this picture?"

"Yes, I do, that's Rosa Lee Kannon."

Joel and Holly's eyes popped wide open as they looked at each other. "Don't you mean Lula Kannon, the daughter?" Holly said.

"Yuh think Ah'm too old tuh know anyone, huh?"

"No Ma'am, I didn't mean it like that.

"Give it here," Millie snapped. "This picture was taken in 1927 on Beaufort's cotton plantation. Even though slavery was over, picking cotton was all we knew how to do. My momma took the same picture in the same spot. Momma and Rosa Lee used to pick cotton from sun up to sun down. My oldest brother, Isiah, was born in that field. Lula and Joseph wasn't born then, but I was. When I was teenager, here come Joseph and Lula. Momma used to make me wash out their cloth diapers and feed'em. On the count of the cotton fields being closer to our home, Rosa Lee kept'em with me. You see the barrette in her hair? She's worn that barrette ever since she grew hair past her shoulders."

"How did she die?"

"I really don't know...by then...I went off to school, became a business woman, got married and moved to Savannah. I heard she died of a broken heart though. You see, after her husband died, she lost everything; her happiness, home and her family."

"You mean, Lula's passing," Holly mildly spoke.

"No, you mean Lula's murder. They never did find the body. Rosa Lee went crazy after that. Some say her soul went to the dark side."

"What about her son, Joseph?"

"You mean, scary boy...well he closed up, too. Folks say he saw what happened...Ole man Creech boys raped her bad and Joseph stood there and watched his sister being taken to her death. That boy was always scared. You could be locked in a room and because he wouldn't know what's behind the door, he wouldn't open it for you. Yes sir, he was something scary alright." Laughing.

Joel and Holly still couldn't get over the fact of how much Rosa Lee resembled Lula as a child. "So, you mean all this time, I've been fighting with Rosa Lee."

"What you say?" asked Millie.

"We moved in the house that was originally Rosa Lee and James Kannon's home. My grandfather and great uncle used to live in her home and when my great uncle Seth died, he willed it to me."

"What you say your name is?" Millie's eyes expanded.

"Joel Lee Keys. Adam Creech was my great grandfather."

"GET OUT! GET OUT! NOW!" Millie shouted, feeling manipulated by her visitors.

Joel desperately answered, "Please...I want to do the right thing."

"Erin, tell these people to go back where they came from."

"Excuse me!" Holly hurt.

"Visiting time is over...please leave."

Millie turned her wheelchair away from Joel and Holly to stare out the window. Joel hesitated to leave the room at first.

"Mr. Joel Lee Keys, go home," Millie sourly spoke.

"My roots are here...this is my home too."

"Then rest in peace," Millie said, with a fading voice.

The slender face met Joel once more in the hallway as he was leaving Millie's room. That same elderly lady he waved to earlier. Something captured their eyes yet again. Smiling without shame, she showed her yellow, broken teeth, keeping her eyes joined to Joel's. Joel forced his frown, flickering sincerity in his eyes then he waved bye.

The sun full of fire seared the grounds of Beaufort. Sweat matted Joel's hair like an uncombed wet bird's wing. As he wiped the sweat off his forehead, he looked up to the sky, purposely blinding himself with the sun rays. "Well, at least we know now, after all these years the Creech family's evil still lives on."

"Actually, we've known that already. Rosa Lee wasn't going to let you forget it," Holly said.

"I don't get it...why did my Aunt totally go off on you and who is Rosa Lee? What does the girl in that picture have to do with your grandfather and great uncle?" Erin asked.

"They raped and tortured this woman's daughter."

"You mean Rosa Lee's daughter, Lula?" Erin asks, appallingly.

Holly looked both worried and distraught as she looked at Erin. "There were strange things happening in the house. Joel and I thought that if we did some family research on his family, as well as Rosa Lee and Lula, then maybe we could find out what really happened and correct it."

"You know what happened. How could you correct something so wicked?" Erin asked, as though she had an awful taste in her mouth.

"We just have to find a way," sighed Joel, shrugging his shoulders. "One day, I will have children and my children may want to visit their ancestors' birthplace...and they too will fall into a deep sleep."

Twenty

Erin was back in the room with Millie.

"What happened to Lula, Aunt Millie, and how come Rosa Lee didn't help her own daughter?"

"Who said she didn't help Lula. Speak not what you don't know and ask what you want to know."

"Well, what happened to Lula?"

"I don't know, but I do know that Rosa Lee made sure Lula was cared for."

"So, Rosa Lee wasn't evil?"

"No baby *gurl*. The hole in her heart was so deep, she drowned in it. You know how sometimes when darkness clouds your thoughts and clarity isn't normal anymore. Well, Rosa Lee's light went out and she couldn't find her way back."

"If Joel is trying to do the right thing, why not help him?"

"'Cause, honey, Joel can't make it right."

"Why not?" Erin was curiously wondering.

"Joel's blood line cast the first stone of evil upon Rosa Lee's family and the last one has to make it right."

"Whatever happened to 'I'm sorry'? At least he wants to make it right. Besides, Aunt Millie, Joel didn't do anything wrong; it was his sick grandfather and great uncle, and great grandfather."

"That doesn't matter!" Millie shouted. "Your blood line will follow you beyond your grave. Joel may not have an evil bone in his body, but he inherits the troubled hearts of his family."

"His family is gone...he's the last one!" Erin shouted back.

"Let these people alone. You can't help them."

"Aunt Millie, please!" Erin softly appeals.

Twenty-One

Perfectly shaped, the sun was falling behind the horizontal line at the edge of the earth. Unaware of Joel and Holly's discovery, Joseph stood at the end of the rigid dock where Lula exhaled and inhaled her last moments of life. The pores from his wrinkled face absorbed the salty ocean, while mosquitoes sucked his blood freely. He looked up to the blank sky in tears. In his mind his words flowed fluently.

"God, you created the heavens and the earth. The earth was naked, and darkness was on the face of the deep, and your spirit moved over the face of these waters. You said let there be light and there was light; you separated that light from darkness. You said, 'come together in one place'. And here I am, standing before You on dry land, while the seas You've created became witnesses to the darkness of this land." Joseph staggered inches forward and dropped to his knees, weeping for forgiveness, eyes stinging. "Ah'm so sorry...Ah wuz scared...Ah wuz scared, please take me now. Ah can't live lak dis no mo'. Lula Ah'm sorry, please take me wid you."

As Joseph wiped his tears away, he had just enough clear sight to notice a pair of eyes watching him in silence from below the water. Joseph slowly dropped his hand from his wet face and took a closer look. The eyes were polished oak brown with highlights of amber, and the neatly arched eyebrows complemented the round face. The face was clearly bronze, not one blemish to view, the lips were wholly shaped and smooth, as though they were faultlessly painted brick red.

"Lula Ah let dem kill yuh," Joseph wept. "Ah'm so sorry, I dint protect yuh...I don lived wid dis in my heart fo' sixty-fo' years. Killed me uh hundred times over...Ah can't take it no mo...why yuh left me heah?" A mild wave moved towards the foot of the dock. Joseph never took his eyes off the rippling water. Dazed and frozen solid, he saw his mother, Rosa Lee standing before him, smiling. "Momma, Momma is dat you?" Crying interrupted his sobbing.

"Don't cry, son, your time on this land was good." Joseph continued to look down, not afraid.

"Lula's spirit has come back and she's full of rage, Momma," he sobs.

"Lula's spirit never left. She breathes."

Stunned by Rosa Lee's words, his whining turned into trembling.

"I don't understand," Joseph gasps. Suddenly, within the flick of an eye, Rosa Lee was gone. Joseph hurriedly bent down to a crawling position, leaned forward into his reflection mirrored by the ocean, and began to panic. Uncontrollable feelings of fear surged through Joseph. He reached down to the water with his right arm and swept the surface with his hand, paddling the water as though Rosa Lee was hiding underneath.

"Joseph...Joseph," a whispering voice came from behind. Joseph's body stiffened. Scared to death to turn around, he squeezed his eyes shut, then opened them, thinking that this may be a dream.

"Joseph, stand up and look at me when I'm talking to you! Haven't I always told you to listen to mother?" It was the evilest voice Joseph had ever heard. Joseph, weary, because he was certain that it wasn't the voice of his mother, began to tremble. Rising off his knees, never looking straight ahead, he looked up at the sky, shivering. In the back of Joseph's mind, he was thinking his punishment had finally come.

"My son, don't be afraid."

"Youse not mah momma!" Joseph shouted.

"Why you forsake me now when you spoke of sincerity seconds ago." A roaring atrocious clamor of rage rolled over to him. "I said look at me when I'm talking to you!"

Joseph could no longer control his ability not to look. His head automatically turned, facing the blasted anguished voice. Eyes and mouth wide open, he took one step back to the edge of the dock in fear. He made an effort to catch his breath and then squeezed his eyes shut again, as tight as he could, then opened them in dismay. Joseph was hoping that when he opened his eyes, 'it' would be gone.

"No Momma, dis can't be you." Sobbing.

"Joseph, it's me...the time has come to take back what's rightfully ours. No one will rest until deliverance comes and evil has met my justice. Your father's acres of heritage were stolen by the sinful hands of evil and greed. Your sister's demise tragically delivered innocence with an unknown face. Now evil will come upon those who share the blood of the ones who first shed this darkness upon my family."

Joseph stood paralyzed. The beautiful bronze structure had turned into a three-hundred-pound dark-faced, sloth-looking thing that hypnotized Joseph with words of petty vengeance. "Do you think I was going to sleep forever in the grave you've prepared for me?" Laughing. "Do you think I was going to let ole man Creech and his sons get away for what they did to my family? My husband, your father, my daughter, your sister - their legacy that was theirs to live and breathe was stripped away from them as though they were nobody!" In a scolding voice as Rosa Lee lashed out. "Your father and his father, and his father before him, worked these 72 acres, beaten down to the bones, stripped of their voices and made to feel less of what God has made them. Your father and I descended from blood where green pastures filled the earth. Land that birthed plentiful and raised goodness. A place where secrets were never told and untold secrets were like gold. Then one day, the sun stopped giving birth and the moon was the only white thing you could see. Our blood confronted the evil mind and evil hands that shawled our intimate souls, but they did not know that our intimate spirits followed." Laughing. "It wasn't enough that ole man Creech's deceitfulness caused us humiliation and shame, but his sons destroyed my daughter's destiny and her will to breathe, to smile, to be seen or touched."

"Momma, what happened to Lula?" sobbed Joseph.

"The ocean loves your sister and she loves the ocean and its deep. Our ancestors' adore Lula – they weren't going to let her drown. That's why she loved this dock so much, it was a peaceful power given to her heart. That day you pulled Lula from the water, the spirits had swarmed around her, protecting her."

"You took Lula in the room and I never saw her again," Joseph bravely interrupted.

"Don't weep for Lula. Weep for your friend, Joel Lee Keys."

"Momma, he didn't do anything," he said as tears dripped down.

"He should have never stepped foot on this land," shouted Rosa Lee. "Go to the grave you've dug for me and take the soil that rests upon me and find your sister. Only the last soul can save him now!"

It was past eleven P.M. and Joel had walked miles – pacing back and forth in the living room a hundred times. He was tired and his nerves had paled him. Even though his body was tired, he knew he could not sleep. The mood was quiet but anxious, knowing that Joel's battle with Rosa Lee was about to come face to face once more.

Rosa Lee's voice drowned in Joseph's head, a dark, wicked voice that was so unrecognizable, nothing like his mother's tone. He stood at the window, gazing out towards the opening of another sunrise morning coming up over the land. Every now and then, Carmen turned up her dark brown eyes to stare at Joseph's ever-changing expressions, watered down by his sweat. She switched her eyes to look at Holly, then Adrian and then Joel. It was as though she were waiting for a verdict to come down. Trembling emotions were overcome by the inspiration to think and the ability to converse out loud.

Finally, Joseph, scared shitless, got the nerve to make a move. He cut Joel off in his 100 mile walk. "Joel, there's something you should know."

"What, Joseph?" Joel slowed down his walk to listen.

"Llll...Lula." It was like Joseph went mute and was trying to speak for the first time. "Lula talks to Momma all the time."

Everyone's eyes traced each others' with unbelievable speed.

"You mean, the living communicates with the dead."

"All dis time, Ah thought mah sista wuz dead," Joseph said.

"Joseph, what exactly happened when you pulled Lula out of the water?" asked Joel.

"Soon as Momma heard all de screamin', she wuz comin', but couldn't get tuh Lula in time. When Ah pulled Lula from de wader, Ah could'uh sworn she wuz not breathin'."

"What happened after that?"

"Momma got dere after I pulled Lula out. She snatched her out of mah arms and carried her home. She took Lula in de room den locked de door. It wuz de next mornin' befo' momma came out. Ah'd never fo'get de way momma wuz actin'. She wuz grindin' her teeth and talkin' crazy. She shook me so hard...her eyes were comin' outta her head. Momma told me tuh never go in de room...never. Ah'd thought momma went mad and she wuz goin' tuh let Lula's body stay in de room fo'ever. Ah told momma what happened. She grabbed mah face and told me tuh hush, never speak of it again fo' it'll come tuh me next."

"For 'what' will come to you?" Joel asked.

"Darkness fo'ever and never waking up."

"That's why you kept silent for so many years."

"Dat wuz mah punishment fo'not he'pin' Lula."

"Well what happened to Lula?" Holly asked impatiently.

Joseph looked at Joel, worried. "Ah don't know."

"You mean to tell me, you never went in the room?"

Joseph narrowed his eyes, shaking his head no. "Ah finally went in de room after momma died...she wuz gone."

"Somebody has to know where she is!" Adrian interrupted.

Joseph steadily stared at Joel again – this time, he couldn't open his mouth wide enough to talk. The door bell rang. Carmen jumped up from her seat and told Joseph to "hold that thought."

"Joseph, you want to say something?"

Joseph scrambled for his thoughts before he spoke. "Joel..."

"Yes."

"Joel, yuh not..."

"Not what?"

"Yuh not de last one."

"What are you talking about?" The room became silent.

"He's right." Everybody turned their heads towards the voice walking in the room. It was Erin.

"Joel Lee Keys, you are not the last descendant, and you have wrongfully inherited this land."

Joel couldn't even begin to think what was going to come out of Erin's mouth next. Erin searched the room for Joseph and walked towards him, never taking her eyes off him. "Mr. Joseph Kannon."

"Yes."

"My name is Erin Canister and Mildred Canister is my great aunt."

"Millie...Millie, Ah's knows hur."

"Your sister, as you know by now, is not dead. As a matter of fact, she's right here in Beaufort county, where she's always been for seventy-seven years."

"Please take me tuh Millie."

"First, there is something else you should know." Erin turned to look at Joel. "You should not have inherited this land. Between your grandfather and great uncle; they had a daughter. She is the rightful owner." Joel froze.

Amazed at what Erin said, Carmen burst out, "Oh my God, Lula had a child!" She looked at Joseph, "That's why you were never allowed to see her."

Erin continued, "Right. As soon as Rosa Lee found out Lula was expecting, she took her out of the house, and she hid her out during her pregnancy. Rosa Lee passed away as soon as the baby was born, which means that Lula stayed away from home because she was embarrassed, ashamed, and couldn't face the eyes of those she once knew without her mother's company."

"Not to mention, she didn't want to look in ole man Creech's face, either. Damn...damn it!"

"Hold on, Joel, there's more. My aunt raised Lula's little girl."

"What?" Carmen gasped in shock.

"Do you know this person, Erin?" Adrian asked.

"That's the sad part, no I do not. Aunt Millie said the child left home when she found out how she came into this world. She started asking questions about her skin color, why she was lighter than her school mates and everyone else who lived around her. Aunt Millie waited until she got old enough to understand, but the truth sometimes weighs on your heart. A month after that, she vanished, never heard a word from her after that."

"Maybe that's why Joel inherited the land, because she couldn't be found," Carmen said.

"Maybe, but the fact remains...as long as this land is heir property, Rosa Lee will never wake up; you will visit the deep with her as long as you and your descendants sleep here," Erin said, looking at Joel.

Joseph murmured to himself slightly, as he remembered his unexpected encounter with his mother, but it was loud enough for everyone to hear him. "Dat tragedy wid an unknown face is mah sista's chile, mah niece, mah fambly...out dere all alone."

"She has a name," replies Erin. Everyone's face was front and center and nothing was going to stop them from hearing what Erin was about to say next. Then she said, "Elizabeth."

Some of the questions had disappeared, and Joseph managed to disguise a smile freely. He broke up the silence by walking over towards his homely recliner and grabbed his cap, then pulled out a shovel from behind the door. "Erin, please take me to Millie, she knows where Lula is."

"It's after midnight."

Joseph took a deep breath and said, "Please."

Erin agreed to take Joseph to Millie. Before Joseph walked out of the house, he looked back at Joel and said, "Don't fall asleep."

Twenty-Two

A couple of hours passed and the house was silent. Suddenly, Carmen spoke. "Why is it...you think you can get away with something without it ever coming back to bite you in the ass?"

"Yeah and when it comes back to you...Look out!" Adrian chuckled in a serious manner.

Joel couldn't help but feel responsible for everything that happened, including Elizabeth's conception. Hesitantly, Joel asked to speak to Adrian alone. "I never once thought that I was better than anybody else. It didn't matter if they were black, white, yellow or green. I never mistreated anyone. I was taught to treat people the way I wanted to be treated. You're my best friend and I can't even look you straight in the face now without you thinking bad about me."

"Hold on, partner. You never did anything to me and I'm not ignorant." Adrian firmly held up Joel's shoulders and looked into his weary eyes with genuineness. "You're like the big brother I never had. That's funny...I always wanted to know my family and here you are, regretting knowing yours."

"I wish I could go back in time and make things right," Joel said.

"You can't, so now you have to move forward for your generation and generations to come."

Out in the living room, Holly and Carmen sat quietly, reflecting on the events that took place. Holly was thinking how 'prejudice' visited Joel without warning and how it came back to relive itself from dead years. In that moment, she took inventory of her character.

"Carmen, when I was in the fifth grade, almost every day, I used to take pencils off my teacher's desk when he would step out of the classroom. They were always sharpened just right. When I was in college, I used to date this football player; his name was Robert G. Smith, oh what a hunk. I caught him cheating on me, so I poured sugar in his gas tank...that Porsche wasn't going anywhere. I know this is nothing compared to what's going on, but do you think that's why I can't seem to find anything to write with when I need to, and that is why I always have car problems?"

Carmen giggled at Holly. "Well then, if that's the case, I'll never find a pen or pencil to write with and that's why I'm walking and not driving." They laughed. Carmen heaved a lengthy sigh then got up to look at Rosa Lee's picture. "Holly, her sleepless soul seeks revenge on the dead's living relatives. The evil that was done to James and Lula can't let her turn the other cheek, so to speak. Ole man Creech's blood line will drip this nightmare until Rosa Lee's broken heart can learn how to forgive again. The thought of knowing her grandchild's blood is mixed with the Ole man Creech's is really why she seeks retribution."

A tear dripped off Carmen's face as she clutched Rosa Lee's picture against her breast. It was as if Carmen knew without a doubt that a pathetic justice emptied Rosa Lee's stomach, and her plight for integrity was killed in cold blood a hundred times over. Carmen continued to gawk at Rosa Lee's mirror image in the photo, and then she realized Rosa Lee's eyes were upon hers. Carmen didn't let fear take over. Whatever message that was about to be revealed, she allowed herself to receive it. Carmen envisioned Rosa Lee standing in the shallow water of the Atlantic, looking up at the moon. She turned to the shore, hinting with her index figure for someone to come with her. Carmen could not see that person, but Rosa Lee wanted

170

them to follow her. Carmen faintly closed her eyes then opened them again.

"Oh my God! Holly, Rosa Lee was buried on land. She wasn't buried in the deep."

"What does that mean?" Holly asked.

"Joseph told us his family found freedom in the deep."

"Yeah, but they drowned themselves to keep from being in bondage."

"Yes, Holly, don't you see, as long as their blood lives on this land, they will never die in peace. They will only go into a deep sleep and their dreams will live out among the dead buried on land. Ole man Creech and his sons are buried on land; since Joel shares the same blood line and as long as he lives on this land, his blood is a 'fresh' kill for revenge."

"That's why Gabe and Seth, couldn't live in James' house, and that's why Joel couldn't live here. She's getting revenge through her dreams on land."

"Something tells me that's why Joseph took the shovel."

"We have to get Joel and Adrian and go."

"Go where?" Holly saw Carmen's look.

"To find Rosa Lee."

The early hours of morning continued to pierce the air with a moderate chill, and the waves kept the Atlantic Ocean awake. Back on land, Joseph was down on his knees once again. Only this time, he was digging up his mother's grave. Snot hung down from his nostrils, like rubber cement glue. His soiled denim overalls were faded blue, now a drenched dark blue plastered to his skin. Diligently shoving the dirt over his shoulders, he noticed a shaft of light shining towards his direction. The glare forced him to stop shoveling.

Wiping his stinging eyes with the back of his dirty sleeve, he was able to get a better view of the light coming his way. As the gleam of light shifted, it was Joel, Holly, Adrian and Carmen. Joseph acknowledged their presence with a quick look and continued to dig. He finally tapped down on the wooden casket he had built with his bare hands for his mother, made from timber that he'd gathered from the side of the road. He lined it with cotton hand-picked from the field and white sheets hand-stitched with Rosa Lee's fine embroidery.

Surprisingly, Rosa Lee's body laid undead for over half a century. Her skin was unsullied and her dress was still as white as the day it was first put on her body. "Momma, tell me what you want me to do now."

Carmen stepped closer to the opening of the grave and said, "She wants to go to her rightful burial place."

Joseph strangely looked at Carmen with contempt. "I don da bes I could."

"Joseph, where is James' grave?"

Joseph pointed, "Right here."

Joel and Adrian took the shovel from Joseph and started to dig up the grave marked 'James Kannon'. The casket was empty. Joseph was dumbfounded and didn't understand what was going on.

Carmen walked over to Joseph and told him, "Your father is not buried on land. He is buried in the waters that overlook his front porch, and Rosa Lee will not go in peace until she is with him."

"I saw mah father go in de ground." A little angry.

"You probably did. But when no one was looking, he went to the deep."

"How?"

"Rosa Lee."

Joseph's eyes became watery and started to reminisce. "One evenin' Ah saw momma in de shallow wader cryin' and cursin' heaven. She was punchin' the wader wid her fis and screamin', 'Ah'm not ready yet, Ah'm not ready yet.' When I closed mah eyes fo' a quick second and opened dem, Ah saw somebody else standin' in de wader. Ah couldn't make out who it wuz. All dey did wuz stand dare, not movin', jis' lookin' at momma. I wanted to get closer to look. Ah went tuh get off mah knees, dey were gone." Joseph sighed and shook his head, wishing he could get more memory back of that somewhat forgettable night. He could still hear the vile cries of his mother's anguish. Inconsolably, he walked back across the graves towards Rosa Lee's unmoving body. Heartfelt from the pits of his soul, he and the others gathered around the restless sleeping flesh in the blackness of the night.

Joseph eyeballed Adrian, "Please help me get momma's body outta here."

As Adrian pulled to lift, he nearly peed in his pants. "Where are we taking her?"

"Home."

Twenty-Three

The restored house that lay on the shoulders of the Atlantic, not much wider than a bungalow, was opened to the lady of the house once again. Rosa Lee's body lay on the dining room table in the middle of the floor, as though it were resting in the State's Rotunda for spectacle view. The dining room was cozy and blended with just enough light. The ocean could be heard breathing and no other echo was able to interrupt the still peace encircling the room at that moment.

Joel, Holly, Carmen and Adrian were standing side by side, hands joined in fellowship.

"Well, what do we do now?" asked Adrian.

"We wait."

"Wait for what? Wait for her to wake up and kill me," Joel whispered.

Joseph dug into his front pocket and pulled out a hand full on soil that came from Rosa Lee's grave. He graciously sprinkled the soil on top of her body from top to bottom. Joseph stared hard at Rosa Lee, then spoke with force, "Joel, your nightmare ends t'night."

"How do you know that?" Joel's tone of voice was weary.

Silence enclosed the room airtight. Carmen looked at Joseph slightly, pursing her mouth before she spoke, "Because Lula has forgiven your bloodline."

Joel sincerely looked at Joseph, who said, tears dropping, "Joel, I'm sorry. Please tell me what you want me to do?"

"Nothin'." An old crackling voice came forth in the room. Lula, Erin and Aunt Millie walked in the dining room.

Joel's eyes stood at attention. "You're the lady I saw in the nursing home."

"You dat man I saw at de nursin' home," Lula said, smiling.

Joel glued his eyes to Lula, keeping her presence in consideration with the highest respect. Lula took small steps towards Rosa Lee's body, "Joel, Ah have tuh 'pologize tuh yuh. Hate is curable only if it wants to be cured." She finally made her way to Rosa Lee, breathing down on her and looking at her with admiration.

Joseph teared up and moved beside his sister. "Lula, dis is all mah fault."

"Naw, Joseph. Dis wuz nobody's fault."

"If Ah wuzn't so scared," Joseph said, weeping.

"Even if yuh would have helped, yuh would have been dead and momma would still do whut she's doin' nah. Momma didn't do dis 'cause of you or me, she did it 'cause she let so much heartache build inside her, dat peace had nowhere tuh go."

Joel quietly stepped behind Lula and Joseph. "Lula...Joseph. Sixty-five years ago, my great grandfather stole something from your father, and I want to give it back to you." Joel glanced at Holly and Holly pulled out a manila folder from a soft brown leather briefcase sitting in the corner on the floor. Holly hurriedly handed it to Joel. Joel reached inside the folder, pulled out a land deed and the original hand written receipt that ole man Creech found near James' lifeless body. "I know it has been over sixty years." Joel sadly looked at Lula. "I can't take back what Gabe and Seth did to you, but whatever you want..." Joel could barely finish his sentence through the shameful tears.

"Ah want yuh to be uh good man."

"I'm so sorry," Joel continued to drown in his tears.

Millie's voice floated to Joel in the midst of his forgiving. "Joel, we all have hearts. It's whether or not we obey what's right in our hearts. There are those who speak rightfully from the heart, but do they do like they speak? God is coming back for all his disciples. He's going to know who one is and who acts like one."

Joel slightly sniffed up the clear mucous running down his nose, back up through his narrow nostrils. "Miss Millie, I have to start from somewhere and I choose to start here and now, on the ground that laid out my destiny." Joel continued to hand over the deed to Lula and Joseph. "This is your land and here is your father's deed. I'm ashamed and I can tell you this, I will never take anyone or anything for granted as long as I live."

Lula clutched Joseph's hand firmly and said, "It's time. It's been real nice knowin' ya'll, but me and momma gettin' ready tuh go home nah. Daddah's waitin' on us."

Joseph sadly looked at Lula. "Why yuh hafta tuh go?"

"Joseph, Ah've been gone uh long time – Ay'm jis' here tuh get momma."

Joseph lifted his wet eyelashes, "Take me witcha."

"It's not yo' time, mah deah brother. Yo' day is comin', be ready. Until then, breathe wuh'ever God gives yuh."

Lula turned around to walk out the dining room. Every window in the house shot open at the same time with a tremendous force, blustering winds intruded with furious strengths, uplifting everything that wasn't nailed down. The walls were crying blood, mixed with vaporous bodies in chains. These vaporous bodies were covered with slashes and keloid markings and their eyes stayed closed.

Fear swelled in the veins of Joel, Holly, Adrian, Carmen and Erin. All eyes switched back and forth at every rapid movement the house made.

Holly tightly squeezed Joel's arm. "Joel, I'm scared."

"Me too."

Lula walked to the front door and turned to Millie, "Thank yuh fuh everythin' yuh heah...tell mah..." Right then and there, Millie reached for Lula's hand, gripping it like two sisters were taught to care for one another in times of need. Lula was able to talk clearly now, "Tell her I love her."

"She knows it...she knows it. She knows you are her mother." Millie let every tear drop fall between the wrinkles in her face then hugged Lula enough to last.

While Joel, Holly and Adrian were scared and confounded at the unexpected mischievous spirits in the house, Carmen stayed in the dining room. She stood heavy, like a statue cemented to the floor. A glaring presence took up space before her and lifted life out of her for that moment.

The rippling sounds continued to trample all through the house. In Adrian's panic, he realized that Carmen wasn't near him. He made his way back to the dining room and there, he saw Carmen standing in what appeared to be a trance. Rosa Lee was standing in front of her, smiling, stroking Carmen as though she knew her. Carmen, not knowing why, gracefully extended her hand out to Rosa Lee. Rosa Lee placed her vintage barrette in her hand, and then closed it. Rosa Lee hurriedly detached her gaze of good judgment and walked away. As Rosa Lee walked out of the dining room, she simply turned to look at Joseph. Eyes moistened, he warmly embraced his mother, a feel of affection without an utter.

Joel prepared his fate. His life's reflection played before him like a movie projector, except that it played fast forward. Vocally cut and barely breathing, Joel never once took his eyes off Rosa Lee. Rosa Lee stood in front of him like a freight train coming and Joel was tied to the tracks. She stood tight, staring at him. Her eyes turned crimson and Joel's tears were suddenly burning the white insides of his eyes. A guilty verdict had finally come; not by a man made law, not by a judge, but by a point in time. It was as though 'darkness came into light' in a matter of seconds.

Rosa Lee reserved her presence before Joel – the distance between their bodies generated a response of understanding. And that's exactly what Joel did. He understood Rosa Lee and that was all he had to do, and then she walked away.

Rosa Lee and Lula tasted the salty sea with gladness as the early night wind caressed their faces. Slowly walking the sandy path towards the awakening ocean, hand in hand, they never looked back at the land that locked their dreams underground. Neither grievance nor heartbreaking emotions were carried out to the deep. Peace was all they had.

Twenty-Four

The last words on the gardenia florid stationery read '...Sincerely with love and care.' Emotions ran past normal blood flow with some hostility and some curiosity, as she sat back and rubbed her fingers across her dripping eyes. Elizabeth wrapped her arms around her chest and looked up to the painted white-splashed ceiling. *"God I always needed you, but I need you more so than ever, now."*

She never thought this day was going to come, at least not in her days of living. Relatives she knew absolutely nothing about and people who were mentioned to her as a little child were a long-ago memory – not anything else. She crunched the letter in her fist, so afraid to know the past and so desperately wanting to keep what she had now. She fought the unknown misery disrupting her mind.

Twelve minutes of pondering passed. She got up from her chair and walked to her bedroom. Elizabeth opened the closet door and found her way through the hanging garments to the back, to an old black trunk that had accompanied her since childhood. As she knelt down, she consoled herself and prepared to meet life's unexpected assessment of her character.

She sniffed and held a photograph of her husband and son in one hand, and a photograph of a woman who gave birth to her in the other. "I never should have been born," she whimpered aloud.

Then a deep voice said, "Yes, you should have." John, Elizabeth's husband, knelt down behind her, holding her shoulders. "Because without you in my life, I wouldn't be who I am today."

"Who am I?" she said, crying.

"You are a beautiful human being, a loving wife, a magnificent mother and soon to be grandmother."

Elizabeth slowly faced John. "When I found out how I was conceived, I threw up for days. I walked with my face down, always hiding these hazel eyes and keeping my hair nappy just so I could fit in...but fit in where?" Laughing and crying. "Black people thought I was too good and white people didn't think I was good enough. I wasn't dark enough, I wasn't light enough. Never mind that I came from some white boys who loathed blacks and raped a black girl. It was two white boys who unloved themselves and raped a black girl," she said, between sobs and dripping tears. "The world sees me as a bastard. I'm a bastard, me, John."

Elizabeth regained control of her tears. "No! They're the bastards, not me! I always had to make sure I was better than everybody else. I thought if I could hide my sinful birth, I would be okay. I didn't want anything that looked like the south touching or reminding me..."

"Honey that was a long time ago. I'm sure what happened to you happened to many young girls back in those days—black, brown, yellow and white. And it happened all over the world, not just in the south. You were not the only one born out of an immoral tragedy."

Elizabeth's skin toned was turning from camel to red. Her sniffles got louder then became uncontrollable. She released the tears in her chest, "John, I don't care. It happened to me and I hate it, I hate it!" Elizabeth swiftly stood and ran out of the closet, leaving John on his knees. John leaned forward in the trunk and noticed the letter. John picked it up and read it.

> *Dearest Elizabeth,*
> *Please don't disregard this letter.*
> *I know you may think less of me for*

who my fore-parents were, please do
not let that stand in the way...

John stood with the letter in his hand and went to Elizabeth, "Honey, I think we should go."

"I don't want to go." Sobbing.

"You know what? I think you truly want to go, but you are fearful and scared to face anyone, or anything, that resembles the place you came from. Do you realize there are people out there who have generational curses in their life due to disobedience? The only thing that happened to you is that you were born which was predetermined before the foundations of time. What about Lula? She lost out too – she gave up a mother's gift that could only have been gifted by God, so that you could have a normal life. It wasn't like she planned the rape and wanted to give birth at the age of thirteen. Don't let this invitation signify fear. Let it make you take responsibility and face all your answers you have about your heritage. Be proud of who you are and take charge of your past and be glad that you made it! I've been in love with you since the first day I met you. We've made a good home together. We've grown together, laughed together, cried together, disagreed together, but not listened to one another. We are blessed to have friends from all over the world; Japan, France, Italy, and Spain. Elizabeth our friends love you for who you are. You have opened your heart and mind with us; I know you can do it for them. For nearly forty years of our marriage, you have hidden your mother, your family secrets, and your passage on earth. Now, I ask you, what are you going to do about it?"

Defeating her tears, Elizabeth knew she had to overcome the anger, embarrassment, pain and ugliness that stretched along her veins more so now than ever.

Elizabeth squeezed her cinnamon-green colored eyes open and shut, extending her arms out, "Are we there yet?"

"Next time we're flying," John said.

"I told you to wake me up when you get tired of driving."

"No, that's okay honey."

Elizabeth gazed out the window. "John," Elizabeth said, heartfelt.

"Do we need to make a pit stop?" John asks.

"No."

"Hungry?"

"No."

"Then what?" John peculiarly asks.

"Thank you."

"For what?" John asked quickly, turning his head to Elizabeth and then back to the road.

"For loving me and not mistreating me," she said while making a strenuous effort to stifle the sobs.

John took his right hand off the steering wheel and grabbed Elizabeth's left hand, "Oh honey...THANK YOU for loving me and not mistreating me."

Elizabeth's tiredness was gone. "It feels good to be awake."

www.ingramcontent.com/pod-product-compliance
Lightning Source LLC
Chambersburg PA
CBHW050936120626
46552CB00001B/237